I0672950

This is a work of fiction. Names, characters, places, and incidents are either the product of the author's imagination or are used fictitiously. Any resemblance to actual persons, living or dead, events, or locales is entirely coincidental.

Moolah Publication   www.MoolahEntertainment.com

Author Y. Money   Ymoneytheauthor@gmail.com
Facebook   Ymoney
Instagram   Ymoneytheauthor
Twitter   Ymoneytheauthor

Editor   Meloni (Dope Publishing)

Cover Designer   ChamarTheArtist
                         artbychamar@cgmail.com

Still Breeze Entertainment   Mcbreeze@gmail.com

Acknowledgements

Thank You, God—my Creator—for giving me a creative mind, guidance, and Your blessing.

To my children, the "Triple-A Gang": Atiya, Anthony, and Ahmad.

To my Noah and Genesis' Momma, Money loves you.

To my mom, dad, siblings, and my super large family—thank you all for all of your support throughout the years.

To my man—my one and only love, my Ken-Ken—thank you for the daily push.

Last but not least, to Kelly and Deb—my BFFs for life—I love you! Thank you both for loving me for me ♥

Thank you—everyone—for all of your
love and support!

Preface

There is nothing like having genuine friendship, sisterhood, and a bond that— under any circumstance—cannot be broken. That person with whom you can share your best moments and your most embarrassing ones. That person you can have a fight with and call an hour later, as if nothing ever happened. That person you can trust around your man and share all your intimate details with. That person you wouldn't tolerate anyone disrespecting and wouldn't think twice about kicking ass for. That person who knows your deepest and your darkest secrets with the confidence of knowing her lips will remain sealed. That person who you will forever love and accept just the way they are. Renee and Sheila are exactly the definition of this extremely rare sisterhood, and they call it loyalty.

Just Moved into College

August 1987: Renee and Shelia just finished unpacking, and Pleasure Principle by Janet Jackson was playing on the radio. Renee hung a big 24x36 poster up of Prince on the wall—his body was dripping wet and he only wore a pair of briefs in the shower. She pulled out some sexy lingerie and hung it all around the poster and replaced the white light with a red light.

"Girl we did it! We are finally unpacked and probably have the flyest dorm at Lincoln," Renee said.

"Girl, fly? Oh okay! If that's what you want to call it?" Sheila laughed.

"What the hell you laughing at, Sheila? You don't like the way I decorate?"

"I like it…it just screams, "PLEASE COME AND FUCK ME!"

"Well, what's wrong with that? I do plan on fucking."

"You're not scared?"

"Hell no…I told you, me and Mike Gaines did it in the boys locker room after the championship game."

"What?! No, bitch! You did not tell me that! You told me you two were kissing and freakin'…" Renee tried chime in, but Sheila cut her off with her hand.

You said, "His pants were down, and your cheerleading skirt was up, and that was it." Sheila pointed her finger, getting closer and closer to Renee's face. Renee took a few steps back to keep Shelia from getting in her face.

"You said you guys were close to getting it in, but you stopped because you heard someone come in—that's what the fuck you said!" Shelia was in Renee's face, waiting for an answer.

"Oh…" Renee looked like she was thinking.

"Oh? Bitch, you withheld information from me?"

"No, Shelia, I thought I told you it went in."

"No, bitch, you didn't. That's fucked up, Renee! I thought we were best friends."

"We are, Shelia! You are my girl—the sister I never had. I really thought I told you it went in once we got back into it and continued."

"No, you didn't," Sheila said, disappointed.

"Damn, Renee, I can't believe you held out on me like that."

"I'm sorry, Sheila. I really thought I told you."

Sheila stared at Renee, and there was an awkward silence for about 3 seconds. Sheila folded her arms, let out a sigh, and pulled Renee's arm.

"Well...come on...give me the damn details! Did it hurt?"

"Whew! Yes, it did, but in a good way."

"What the hell is that supposed to mean? Either the shit hurt, or it didn't?"

"I can't believe I didn't tell you this because this conversation feels so repetitive, girl! I know I did."

"Well, who else could you have told this to, besides me?!"

"No one, Sheila! That's why this is so crazy!"

"Yeah, yeah, yeah...come on with the details."

"Alright...while we were grinding, he pulled his pants down and girl! That made his dick start poking me through my cheerleading briefs. It felt like his dick was getting closer and closer to entering my pussy. That shit made me want it! I was so fucking horny and excited. I wanted him to just do it, and put it in me so bad. Hmmm...but then, someone came in. So, he put his hand over my mouth to keep me quiet, and we waited in that position until they left back out. Slowly, he started grinding on me again, so I said fuck it and pulled my cheer briefs to the side to help him get that dick right where it needed to be..."

Renee started singing and talking at the same time, like an opera singer, "Right at the entrance of my pussy hole!"

Renee laughed, holding her hand up to high five Sheila. Sheila rejected it, pulling back and leaving Renee hanging.

"You know what? You're a nasty bitch," said Sheila.

"I sure am. Do you wanna hear more or not?"

"Yeah, yeah, girl...go ahead."

"You act like this is a little too much for your virgin ears or something," Renee said sarcastically.

"Girl, will you finish the damn story!" Sheila said, getting agitated.

"Okay, okay..." she smacked her lips.

"Anyway, girl, he started to get excited and grind faster and faster. The head was right there, poking its way through, but it wasn't quite in yet, and that feeling was driving me crazy! I wanted it more and more, and my pussy was so

3

wet, I thought it was bleeding. The feeling was so amazing. I didn't even give a fuck anymore. All I wanted for him to do was get that dick inside me! Girl, I wanted it so bad. I grabbed his ass and told him, "Fuck me now!" He pushed his dick in me so hard! I mean, rammed it all the way in my pussy! It hurt and felt good at the same damn time. I got confused for a minute. I didn't know if I should scream, pass the fuck out, or fuck him back! He kept going and going. My legs started to shake every time he pushed up inside me. He was whispering all this sexy shit to me, telling me he loves me, and that shit had me to the point of wanting to fuck him back. By then, he was like, 'Oh shit, oh shit' and went into convulsions, and came all over the place—oh…you know what…that is where you must've misunderstood me, Sheila! When I said, 'I wanted to fuck him, but it was too late'… yeah…that's what I think it was, Sheila."

Renee looked at Sheila for confirmation.

"No, bitch, you said you didn't fuck him! I'm not slow."

"Dah…well, actually, Shelia, I didn't fuck him—he fucked me, which means "we"—meaning more than one—didn't fuck. He did all the fucking," Renee shrugged

"Bitch, you need to shut the fuck up with your lying ass before I get mad. I can't believe you didn't share your first time with me. Then got the nerve to be sitting here lying in my face, trying to explain some who-fucked-who shit, as if you didn't fuck. I thought we were best friends!" Renee grabbed Sheila's arm, and Sheila pulled away and sat on the bed.

"Shelia…"

"Don't 'Shelia' me! Let's move on to something else, Renee. I'm done talking about this."

"Damn, Sheila, I'm sorry." Sheila didn't answer or look her way.

"I said, 'I'm sorry,'" Renee said, getting in Sheila's face, giving her a sad, sorry, puppy-dog look to make her laugh. Sheila turned away, trying to hold in her laugh but couldn't. Sheila laughed and pushed Renee out of her face.

"Girl, get out my damn face. I can't forgive you for this one." Renee leaped on top of Sheila and started kissing Sheila all in her face. With every kiss, she said, "I love you, friend."

"Renee! Get your ass off of me," she laughed.

"Forgive me, now!"

4

"No, bitch!" Renee leaped back on top of her.

"Okay, okay, okay. I forgive you!" They both laughed.

"C'mon, Sheila, I'm hungry. Let's get something to eat."

"Yeah, I do feel like walking and checking out the scenery. Let's walk down the road to Hardee's instead of the cafeteria."

"Okay." Sheila and Renee grabbed their Gucci pocketbooks. Renee stopped to look for something.

"C'mon...what you looking for?"

"I'm looking for my gold fingernail. I thought I put it right here on the dresser."

"Oh, I put it in the top drawer. I put it there when you knocked it over putting in your freak light."

"Yeah, you say that now, but wait until you get your first. You're gonna appreciate that freak light," Renee laughed, getting her gold nail out the drawer.

"Got it! Let's go."

As Sheila and Renee walked out of their dorm room, two guys were in the hall talking to two girls in the next room over. One was about 6'1, with a light-skin completion, curly hair, and light eyes. The other one was taller—about 6'4—and had a dark-brown skin tone, medium build, dark eyebrows, a shining, black, curly high-top fade, and black sparkly eyes. Sheila and Renee walked out, passing them standing in front of the dorm next to theirs. Sheila and the guy with the light-skin completion were real obvious with their eye contact. He couldn't help but to see Sheila's fat ass. After taking one glimpse at Sheila's ass, he couldn't hold it in.

"Damn! Her ass is fat as hell in that Adidas sweat suit!" Sheila looked back with a smile and started to switch on purpose.

"What's up?" said the light-skin guy.

"What up?" Sheila replied with a little giggle, as they continued walking.

"Yo, hold up!" called out the light-skin guy. Sheila and Renee paused.

"Don't be talking to other bitches while you're with me!" exclaimed one of the girls they were talking to from the next room. Sheila got serious instantly, as she turned around and power walked toward the girls. Renee grabbed Sheila's arm, but Sheila pulled away.

"I'm not with you, I'm with my man, Dwight, right here," corrected the light-skin guy. Dwight got startled, as he quickly took a few steps forward and grabbed Sheila.

"Whoa, hold up! Where you think you're going?"

"Damn! You fast as hell," said the light-skin guy, grabbing Sheila as well.

"What the fuck you say, bitch?!" exclaimed Sheila.

"Oh hell no! Let her go!" yelled the girl at the door.

"Come on, Kay-Kay. Cut it the fuck out! You always starting shit," said Dwight.

"Yeah, and I can finish it, too!" The other girl in the door grabbed her friend Kay-Kay as well.

"Come on, Kay-Kay. Let that shit go," said Dwight.

Dwight turned around to Sheila and Renee, "Look, I suggest you go ahead. Kay-Kay ain't no fucking joke, and I don't want to see her fuck your pretty face up."

"Oh really? Let that bitch go!" exclaimed Sheila.

"Come on, Pretty…" said the light-skin guy, as he put his arm around her and directed her to go the opposite way down the hall.

"My name is Thaddeus, what's yours?" he asked.

"Why you didn't let me fuck that bitch up?" Sheila responded, disregarding his question about her name.

"Damn, that's a long ass name," Thaddeus joked "You are too cute to be fighting, and I know you have more class than that, Pretty."

"Yeah, yeah…but disrespectful ass bitches like that need to be taught a lesson."

"Yeah, she was off the fucking hook," Renee cut him off.

"Your name is Thaddeus, right?" asked Renee.

"Yeah."

"Well, you know we gonna have to handle that, once we see those bitches again?" said Renee.

"We?" asked Sheila.

"Yes, Sheila, "we." There were two of them. I'm not gonna let you fight them by yourself."

"You two don't have to fight no damn body. Ignore them," Thaddeus interjected, trying to bring calm to the situation.

"It's not that simple. Those bitches are right next door to us. You think we gonna just let that shit go?" asked Renee.

"Again, "we"? Sheila asked, as she got closer to Renee, putting her hands on her hips.

"Renee, you know your scared ass ain't gonna do nothing. I'll handle this."

"Listen…why don't you two just chill the fuck out, talking like you all tough and shit. Now, take my advice before Kay-Kay beat y'alls asses," Thaddeus warned laughing.

"The only way this ass has a chance getting beat, is if it's by a man," Sheila said to his face.

"Mmmm…look, you can't be saying shit like that to a brotha because someone like me can take that statement two different ways." Thaddeus said, getting close up on Sheila, licking his lips and trying to be sexy.

"So, umm…which way are you talking?"

"Hmmm…I guess it's for me to know and you to find out," Sheila said, giggling and walking off, pulling Renee along.

"Sheila, you talk a lot of shit to be a virgin," Renee said.

"Yes, girl, did you see his face while I was flirting with him?" she recalled, laughing.

"Yeah…keep playing with these college boys, and someone is gonna pop that cherry real soon!"

"Renee, did you forget? We are college girls. I'm not scared of no college boys."

"Yeah, whatever. Your ass was scared for me when you found out about my first time, so I know that ass is gonna be scared when it's your turn."

"No, I asked if you were scared. Get your facts right. I didn't say anything about me being scared."

"Whatever, Sheila. You talk a lot of shit. We'll see," Renee laughed, as they continued their walk to Hardee's.

The Football Field

The guys just finished stretching and are running drills and talking trash to one another. Fred is talking trash to Jim.

"Let me see who's gonna be my victim today." He turned around and pointed at Jim.

"Oh, you got jokes today," Jim chuckled.

"I know who doesn't have jokes: your corny ass." All the guys laughed.

"Just wait. You'll see how corny my jokes are when I do my show called *Serious*.

"*Serious*? Are you the fuck serious? Eddie Murphy called his "Delirious," so your biting ass gonna call your shit "Serious"? Fred laughed.

"I told you, your ass is corny. You can't come up with nothing better than that?"

"Naw, that's good shit right there, and that's how you get your foot in the door—with controversy. See how you quickly picked up on that? That's going to have everyone talking about it and comparing me with Eddie Murphy. See, it takes a person who knows the business to think of shit like that."

"Man, you can't compare your corny ass to Eddie Murphy! What the fuck is wrong with you!?!" The coach blew his whistle for drills.

"Come on with your bitin' big ass. I'm gonna shake the shit out of you and hopefully knock some sense into that empty ass brain of yours. Comparing your ass to Eddie Murphy, really? he laughed.

"Don't let me catch your ass on the field because you know your career is gonna be over, right?" asked Jim.

Fred kept fucking with Jim, laughing and teasing him. Jim started to get angry and was not playing anymore.

"That's okay, keep laughing. I'm gonna squeeze the shit out of your dumb ass."

"Awwwww…somebody is mad!" Fred laughed and spoke like a baby.

"Ain't nobody mad, man. Just c'mon! Let's do this shit on the field."

"Wait a minute, hold up. What the hell your ass gonna be playing? Because I'm playing football, and your ass sound like you're gonna be playing wrestling."

Fred sarcastically made his voice deep like Jim's and did a wrestling stand.

"I'm gonna squeeze the shit out of your little ass!" Fred laughed. Jim was not laughing and stared really hard at Fred, giving him the look of death.

"C'mon man, it's just jokes. You of all people should know a joke when you hear one. You're a comedian." Fred looked at Jim for confirmation, but Jim is still stared at him.

"Right?"

"Don't try to soften my ass up now. Get that ass on the field!" All the fellas laughed.

Awww, c'mon Jim! It's like that? I can't joke with you now?"

"Naw bitch, bring that ass on!"

"Oh dude, you're really serious!" Fred said, with a shocked look on his face. "That's fucked up!"

They all get into place to start their drills, and all of a sudden, Fred gets sick.

"Coach! I don't know what the hell I ate, but I gotta shit all of a sudden!"

"Go handle that Fred, but get your ass right back out here on the field," Coach said.

"I don't think that's gonna happen, Coach. This is like the third time. I think it's diarrhea!" As he ran off the field, Jim eyed Fred because he saw right through his bullshit.

"You know I'm still gonna get your punk ass?!" yelled Jim.

"Jim, chill. It's just jokes!" Fred ran off the field, looking back laughing at Jim. They continued with practice. After the first practice drill, Jim looked over—near the bleachers and noticed Renee and Sheila watching them practice.

"Damn, look at Renee's fine ass."

"You still on Renee?" Wendell asked.

"Hell yeah, you can't tell me she ain't fly as shit. I hope she still over there when we're done. I'm getting them 7 digits today."

"And my ass is gonna be right there with you. Sheila fly as shit, too!"

"You on Sheila?"

"Hell yeah, Sheila got a fat ass!"

"Alright. Let's do this." Jim and Wendell continued practicing with the team. Renee and Sheila started yelling out to the boys from the bleachers.

"Come on Wildcats! Y'all better give me something to cheer about this year!"

"Damn, Renee. I don't see how you do it?"

"Do what?"

"Cheer for all these fine ass men and not dive in like it's a damn swimming pool." They both laugh.

"Girl, I can see myself now. When they all pile up on top of each other like that, my ass will be running across the field trying to jump right in, each and every play."

"That's because your ass is horny as hell, and you need some dick." They both laugh.

"Oh, don't worry! I'm gonna get Thaddeus' ass to take care of that."

"Oh shit! What the hell Thaddeus do?"

"Nothing, I just know he's the one. Girl, he gave me butterflies and made everything inside me tingle." She rubbed down from her stomach to her vagina, shivering as if she felt a chill.

"Wheeew! You never felt that before?"

"Yeah, well, I think? Oh girl, I don't know? I think I felt like that with every fine ass nigga I came across."

"Maybe it's because you don't allow yourself time first and don't let things settle in before you just start humping all on them."

"Damn, Sheila! You make me sound like I'm some fuckin whore or something!"

"Well..." Renee said, as she looked the other way.

"Bitch really!"

"Sike, girl! I'm just playing." Sheila started laughing. Renee folded her arms and looked the other way.

"Renee, I'm just playing. Stop taking things so damn serious." Renee kept a straight face.

"Renee, c'mon! Stop it!" Sheila tried to butter her up.

"Uh oh. Here come the fellas, Renee." Renee still appeared to be upset.

"Come on, girl. Chill out with that shit. I said I was only playing." Renee slowed but started to loosen up, giving Sheila a fake smile as Jim and Wendell walked up.

"What's up Renee?" asked Jim.

"Oh wow, hey Jim. What's up?"

"You."

"Me?"

"You heard me. I haven't seen you since graduation.

I'm surprise to see you here. I thought you had a scholarship to Pitt."

"I did. I had one for here as well, and when I found out your fine ass was coming here, my decision was made."

"Yeah, whatever. That's what your mouth says."

"Whatever my ass. I'm serious! You gonna be my wife someday. I promise you that."

"Your wife? Can we get to the "like" stage first?"

"Been there, done that."

"What about me?"

"You'll get there, if you're not already. I even made love to you in my mind a million times already."

"Well, damn! Was I any good?"

"Soft, tight, beautiful, and tasty." Jim licked his lips. Renee flagged him and laughed.

"Man, you are so fuckin' weird and got a lot of game!"

"Nooo, no game here! I'm serious. You can even ask my mom when you finally meet her."

"Your mom?" she laughed.

"Yeah. She's the one who washed all those sticky drawers I messed up every night because of you." They both laugh. You had me busting hard, every night! So, until you really give me some, you have to do my laundry."

"No, the hell I'm not!"

"Yes, you will. I told you, you are going to be my wife." Renee blushed.

"Word? This is by far the weirdest come on ever."

"That's because you're beautiful, and you're different. I'm not your average nigga."

"No, you are crazy as hell and tripping."

"Can I come see you later?"

"Oh, I see you don't waste any time either."

"Why should I? It's not like you don't already know me. I let you slip by me in high school, why waste more time? Besides, I already told you, you're gonna be my wife and that's that."

"I've gotta give it to you, Jim. Your confidence level is through the roof."

"So, when is it a good time for me to come?" Renee still blushed.

"Well, damn. Come through around six."

"Where you at?"

"The new dorms, 31H."

"Sheila, can I come hang out with you when Jim comes over?" Sheila shocked and caught off guard.

"Excuse you? What's your name again?"

"Oh, why you gonna try and play me like that Sheila?"

"Oh yeah, Wendell, is that you? I'm sorry, I didn't recognize you without your girl, Michelle, attached to your hip." Wendell laughed.

"Michelle and I broke up over the summer."

"Broke up? I thought you two were inseparable."

"Yeah, we were, but that was high school. You act like us being together was a problem or something? I thought women like that kind of attention?"

"Yeah, we do."

"So why are you trying to play me like I'm soft or something?"

"Man, nobody trying to play you. I was just joking."

"No, you're not. I think you were jealous. I bet you want what she had."

"Jealous?! Nigga please. Ain't nobody jealous of no damn Michelle!"

"I didn't say of her. I said you want what she had, meaning us, our relationship. I bet with your evil ass you never had no one treat you like that before?"

"Boy, get out my damn face before I fuck you up! C'mon Renee."

"Really, Sheila? It's like that?" Wendell stood there with his arms open as Sheila walked away, ignoring him.

"Alright Jim, Sheila's leaving. I gotta catch up with my girl."

"Alright. You not gonna hold me accountable for their bullshit, are you? I really want to see you later."

"No, I'm not—just don't bring his dumb ass when you come."

"Damn, Renee, it's like that? I wasn't trying to be smart or nothing like that. I was only speaking the truth."

"Yea, yea, yea, nigga…" Renee flagged Wendell away.

"Jim, see you later. Let me catch up with my girl."

"Okay, wifey," Jim turned around quickly to Wendell.

"Damn, man! Thanks for almost messing that shit up for me."

"Man, Sheila is too damn sensitive. I ain't say nothing wrong."

"Really?" Jim gave Wendell a dumb look.

"You told her she was jealous of another woman, and you ain't see nothing wrong with that?"

"That's not what I was trying to say."

"Your ass went to West Philly High, right?" Wendell nodded his head.

"So, you know like I know that Sheila is a fuckin' lose cannon."

"She didn't even give me a chance to finish what I was trying to say. She just started bugging fuck out!"

"I would've bugged out, too! You went a long ass way trying to get your fuckin' point across. What the hell were you trying to say anyway? Because I couldn't even figure that shit out."

"I just wanted her to know she was worth getting all my attention and then some, like I gave Michelle."

"What?" Jim looked confused.

"Well, where in the hell did all that jealous shit come from? You should've just said that shit!"

"I was trying to…"

"What? When? You just gotta say what the hell you gotta say to Sheila. Don't be tryna play mind games and shit. You gonna catch a right fucking hook playing around with her."

"Man, I'll just apologize when I go over there with you later."

"Oh, no the hell you won't! You're not fucking up my shit!"

"I just wanna go over and apologize. I like Sheila, and I want her to know that."

"Well, my name is Bennett, and I'm not in it. You do that shit on your own time." Jim patted Wendell's back and walked away.

"C'mon, man! You're not gonna look out for me? All I want is for you to open this door back up for me." Jim turned around as he was walking away.

"Nope! Now let me get my ass back to my room, so I can get showered and dressed for my wife to be." Jim ran to the dorms.

The Girls
Next Door

Renee and Sheila are watching School Daze on TV.

"Man, I love this movie. This is the reason I wanted to go to college." Sheila turned around to Renee with a puzzled look from what she just said.

"School Daze is your only reason for coming to college?"

"Yup."

"So, furthering your education to survive in this thing called life was out of fuckin' the question?"

"Oh yeah, that too. But look how they made college look so fun. I always wanted to join the light skin sorority and run shit like Tisha Campbell did, with all the pretty girls."

"Wait a minute, bitch! What the fuck you tryna say?"

"Oh no, Sheila, nothing like that…" Sheila cut Renee off, with a quick punch in the mouth.

"Damn Sheila! What the fuck you do that for!?!"

"Call me a Giggaboo again bitch, and I'm going to really whoop your ass!"

"I didn't call you no damn Giggaboo!"

"Yes, you did, you said that shit indirectly."

"When the fuck did I say that?"

"You didn't have to say it, to say it. I watched School Daze too bitch, and you were either a wanna be or a mutha'fuckin' Giggaboo. The light skin girls were considered the "Wanna Bes," and the brown skin girls were considered the "Giggaboos." *Renee wiped the blood from her mouth with a tissue.*

"Well, Sheila, I wasn't saying it like that. Damn! You know what, Sheila?" Renee was cut off by a knock at the door.

"Who is it?"

"Unfinished business, bitch! That's who the fuck it is!"

Sheila ran over to the door, opened it, grabbed Kay Kay by the hair and started punching her in the face. Kay Kay's girlfriend, Trina, jumped in it, jumping on Sheila's back. Renee picked up a broom and started swinging it, hitting everybody. Other girls ran from their rooms to observe the fight. Sheila still punched Kay Kay with Trina on her back. Trina and Sheila screamed ouch because Renee hit them with the broom. Sheila threw Trina off her back and stomped her. Renee mistakenly hit Sheila in the head.

"Ouch, Renee! Put the fucking broom down!" Sheila finishing the girls.

"That's right, get them bitches, Sheila! They don't know who the fuck they fuckin' with!" yelled Tamika. Renee looked around at everybody, still holding the broom, paranoid that someone else might jump in.

"Does anybody else want some? If so, come on now while I'm giving out ass whoopings!"

"That's right, Sheila! Teach them bitches not to fuck with us anymore!" The girls across the hall started to head back into their rooms as Sheila kicked Trina one last time before walking away, leaving them laying there.

"I told her hard-headed ass we went to West together and not to fuck with you because she was going to get her ass whooped, Sheila! But she continued on and kept talking shit about you after you left earlier. I guess a hard head makes a soft ass!" Tamika from the dorm across the hall exclaimed. All the girls laughed on the way back into their dorms, gossiping about the fight. Renee and Sheila started heading back into their room as well.

"Sheila, we are the shit!" Renee said, as she danced and put her hand up to high five.

"We whooped them bitches' asses!"

"We? We who, Renee?"

"Me and You!" Sheila gave Renee a smirk.

"Oh Sheila, you gonna play me like that?"

"Alright girl, I'll give you some credit this time because you did try, but next time open your eyes, bitch, when you come out swinging! I don't know who the hell you were aiming at. You fucked me up with that broom!"

"Oh shit. Sorry, girl! I was hype as shit when I saw that other bitch jump in. I was like fuck that shit. It was not going down like that!" Renee got a wet washcloth and some ice out the fridge to put on Sheila's head.

"Damn, girl! I did fuck you up," she said, feeling a lump on her head.

"I'm sorry. I was just trying to help."

"You sure your ass wasn't getting back at me for punching you earlier?"

"No, girl. I really was trying to help."

"I know. It's okay. My ass is going to be sore as shit tomorrow. This is the time I wish I was home, so I can take a nice hot bath and sit in the tub."

"Yeah, this shower only thing is something I've got to get used to."

"Tell me about it. I guess I'll just stand there and let hot water run down my body."

"Damnit!"

"What?"

"I'm missing School Daze!"

"Oh girl, don't worry about it. You can watch it all you want. I have it on tape."

"Oh, cool! Where is it?"

"In my blue suitcase, that's where all my movies are."

"Yes! I love that movie!" Renee started to go through Sheila's movie collection.

"Oh shit, Sheila! You've got Grease 1 and 2—girl, I love these, too!" Sheila grabbed her robe, towel, and washcloth and headed to get showered, while Renee put School Daze in the VCR and lay down on the bed. About 15 minutes into the movie, there was a knock at the door. Renee jumped up in a panic.

"Aw shit! I hope it's not them bitches again! Who is it?"

"Thaddeus." Renee opened the door.

"What's up? What you doing here?"

"Your girl here?"

"Who? Sheila?"

"Who else?"

"Not at the moment. She's down the hall. You can come back in a sec. She should be back shortly."

"Can I just come in and wait?"

"You know what, sure." Renee responded deviously.

"She's gonna be really surprised when she sees you." Renee smiled as Thaddeus came in looking around.

"Damn, whose sexy ass gear all on the wall?" he asked Renee, laughing.

"Sheila's." Thaddeus' eyes just light up.

"Oh, word?"

"Where's your bul at?" Thaddeus tuned her out and continued to look at the wall.

"Damn, Sheila! She be wearing all this sexy shit?" Thaddeus smiled, as he looked at the wall.

"Did you hear me? Where's your bul?"

"Oh damn, my fault. I don't know where he is. He's probably in his room. Why? You on him or something?"

"No. I thought maybe the two of you were next door, seeing your little girlfriends again."

"Them chickenheads are not our girlfriends."

"So, you came here on the strength of us and not Kay Kay and that other bitch, Trina?"

"Oh, that's the other girl's name? See, you know more about them than I do."

"Mmmm hmmm…"

"I don't give a fuck about them girls. I was just walking my bul over here to see his homies."

"Oh, so you won't take what I'm about to say personally then?"

"Take what personally?"

"The way we had to whoop their asses earlier."

"Who ass you whooped, Kay Kay?"

"Yeah, we whooped both those bitches' asses!"

"Seriously. That shit from earlier escalated to a real fuckin' fight?"

"Yup! It sure did. When we got back, them bitches had the nerve to knock on our door and start tripping. So, they left us no choice but to whoop their asses."

"Man, y'all illing. That shit shouldn't have even gone that damn far. Look at you! You all hype and shit, sticking your chest out like y'all crazy with the hands like that."

"That's because we are! Y'all were talking all that shit, like we were going to get our asses whooped."

"I was just talking shit. That was my bul. He knows them. I don't know them like that. Besides, I thought you two were too cute and had more class

20

than that to be out here fighting anyway." Sheila walked in wearing a robe and a shower cap on her head.

"Oh my God! What are you doing here?" She turned around to hide her face.

"What's up, Sheila?"

"Why are you here? Is it because of the fight earlier?"

"No, I actually just learned about the fight. I came to see you. You don't want my company?"

"No…I mean, yes. Well, not like this. Stand outside for a minute, while I get dressed."

"Why? You look beautiful the way you are."

"I don't have no clothes on, Thaddeus." Thaddeus smiled.

"Exactly."

"Boy, please, I have a shower cap on. Get your ass outside."

"You're still beautiful." Sheila started blushing and turned around."

"Out!" Sheila pointed her finger at the door, while holding her towel up with her other hand.

"Okay. Just don't forget that I'm standing out here. I know how long it takes for you women to get dressed." Sheila quickly started getting dressed.

"Girl, why the hell you didn't tell me he was here?"

"I wanted to surprise you."

"Not looking like this."

"Girl, that shit is sexy."

"Wearing a shower cap, Renee?"

"No, I ain't say all that, but you in the robe and him standing there, knowing you don't have anything on underneath, is sexy!"

"How the hell do you know?"

"I know. Girl, I read books and watch freaky movies to learn about men and what they like. We gotta keep up with the Kay Kay and Trina type bitches. Those girls are freaks, Sheila! We can't be clueless when it comes to pleasing a man, or we'll be chasing their asses right back to them freaks. Men want women to know what they want and what they are doing."

"I thought men wanted virgins, too?"

"Only to say they had it first."

"Hmmm…well, what do I need to do because I don't want to seem inexperienced when I finally get with Thaddeus?"

"Girl, I'll school you on everything, just hold off until I do."

"Okay, I'm dressed. Open the door, and let him in."

"You still have the shower cap on your head."

"Oh shit, wait!" Sheila quickly brushed her hair back into a ponytail.

"Okay, now." Renee opened the door for Thaddeus.

"What's up, Thaddeus? You know I'm surprised to see you here? Did you come to chew my back out for whooping Kay Kay and Trina's asses?"

"Naw. I told you, I just found that shit out now. Your girl told me all about it though. I can't believe that shit even went that far."

"I can't believe it either, but that bitch asked for it."

"Well, I don't wanna hear about my lady fighting and shit like that anymore."

"Oh…Trina's your lady?"

"No, you are." Sheila started blushing but tried to play it off.

"Oh wow, when did this happen?"

"When you told me it's for me to know and you to find out. I'm here to find out, but out of respect, I should make you my girl first."

"Hmmm. Your girl? You don't even know me."

"I'll find all that out and then some, spending time with you. You find out something new about a person all the time, even if you been with them for 10 years. You never truly know a person, so I figure if we do this now, it will give us a jumpstart on our relationship starting from the beginning. Hopefully, later down the line, we'll graduate together as husband and wife."

"Sheila, this nigga got game like Jim! I'll give it to you Thaddeus, you are good!" Renee clapped.

"Renee, mind your business."

"Yeah, mind your business, Renee. This is between me and Sheila."

"I know you didn't just tell her to mind her business."

"I was just repeating what you said, trying to help you out."

"Oh, you buggin'!" Sheila put her finger up at Thaddeus.

"You can't talk to her like that. Only we can do that shit to each other, no outsiders."

"See, that's what I'm trying to fix. I want to become an insider. Literally…" Thaddeus smiled, flirting with Sheila as she tried to play off blushing.

"Renee, you are so right. He got game. Well, at least you think you got game, but I see right through all that shit you talking," she said, looking at Thaddeus.

"I'm not trying to play you. I'll prove it to you."

"How?"

"No sex. I will never ask you for none. I'll wait until you are ready, with no question."

"No sex?"

"Nope. It's all about getting to know you, shorty." He walked up close to her face and softly kissed her lips.

"Did I say you can kiss me?" Sheila flirted.

"No." Thaddeus came up even closer, so their bodies touched. He looked her in her eyes and kissed her again.

"Is that a problem?" Sheila kissed him back this time.

"No." She looked him in his eyes.

"Mmmm…" Thaddeus kissed her again, sticking his tongue in her mouth. He finished it with a gentle suck on her bottom lip. Their chemistry was interrupted with a knock at the door. Renee walked over to answer.

"Who is it?"

"Jim." Renee opened the door.

"What's up, wifey!" Thaddeus whispered to Sheila.

"I didn't know. She went with Jim."

"He's delusional, like you."

"Oh, you got jokes. I'll show you who's being delusional alright." He palmed her butt. Shelia jumped away, laughing.

"Damn. You are right on time." Renee said, sarcastically. Renee opened the door to invite him in.

"Girl, I've been standing out front for about ten minutes, waiting to knock on this damn door. I couldn't wait to see my wife."

"Man, you need to stop with all them damn lies and chill with all that wifey stuff."

"I call it as I see it." He looked around.

"Oh, snap! Thad, what's up?" He walked over to shake Thaddeus' hand.

"What's up, Beast? You kill anybody on the field yet?" They laughed.

"Naw, not yet. I was going to get this little fucker today who got under my skin, but his ass pussied out. I'll get his little ass tomorrow though, trust me." They laughed again.

"I know you dunking on niggas. I don't even have to ask! They can't stop your ass for shit! You know you gonna be a problem for #23 when you get to the NBA, right?"

"Even though that's my idol, I would love that challenge!" The girls watched them talk as they went back and forth. What Renee was hearing about Jim intrigued her.

"Husband, Thaddeus makes you sound dope as shit!"

"What? You don't know!?" Thaddeus gave Renee a crazy look.

"This man is definitely going to the NFL! They were trying to draft his ass last year in high school. You better school her, bro!" They laughed and did this crazy handshake. Jim stopped laughing and looked around.

"Damn, y'all freaks!"

"Not me...Renee!" Sheila exclaimed.

"She said that was your stuff."

"Oh, no she didn't!" Shelia looked at Renee angrily.

"Sheila, I said sike!"

"No, she didn't, baby. She said each one of these sexy outfits represented every victim you whipped. She was telling me all this freaky stuff you did to them and..." Sheila cut him off.

"No, she didn't! She knows I'm a virgin. Ooops!" She covered her mouth really quickly and turned to avoid eye contact with Thaddeus.

"You're a virgin?"

"Yes, unfortunately."

"You don't kiss like no virgin."

"That's because I've got a lot of experience in that. That's about as far as I go." Thaddeus grabbed her hand.

"Come here, I'm proud of you. That's nothing to be ashamed about."

"I thought because I was inexperienced sexually, you wouldn't want to talk to me?"

"Girl, you must don't know. Every man on campus would be knocking on your door if they knew that. Every man wishes they were their girl's first." Thaddeus bit his bottom lip and looked at Sheila as if she was his next meal. Jim butt in.

"Baby, this your freaky shit?"

"Yeah, Jim, why?"

"Oh, don't get me wrong. I'm cool with it. I love me a freak!" He stuck his chest out.

"You act like you are going to benefit from it or something?" Renee said sarcastically.

"Two freaks in the bed…whew! I smell nothing but trouble!" Jim got close up on Renee.

"Damn. What happened to your lip, baby?"

"Long story. Sheila hit me by accident."

"Let me kiss it for you." Jim tried to kiss Renee.

"Nigga please. Chill the fuck out!" Renee mugged him. Jim started talking like Al Pacino from the movie Scarface.

"Okay. You don't like me now, but you'll love me tomorrow." Everybody laughed. Jim grabbed a pillow and lay across Renee's bed.

"Well, damn! Make yourself at home, why don't you! You comfortable?" Renee said sarcastically again.

"No, I can use a pop, a sandwich, and some chips. Go ahead, and hook that up for me, baby." Renee rolled her eyes at Jim but got up to make him a sandwich.

"Damn, how you even know we got food?" She walked to the fridge. "We only have bologna."

"That's cool."

"You want anything, Thaddeus?"

"Yeah, throw me a pop." Renee threw him a pop. Sheila invited him to sit on her bed.

"Put on a movie or something." Thaddeus requested. Sheila got up to find a movie. As she backed away from the TV, "The Godfather" came on the screen.

"Damn Sheila! You must be trying to keep my man Thad here all night? You made sure you found the longest movie you could find." Everybody laughed.

"Shut up, Jim. Maybe it's a hint." Sheila flirted with her eyes at Thaddeus.

"You don't have to give me no damn hint," Thaddeus replied, flirting back and licking his lips.
"As a matter of fact, I think I forgot something in my room. You should walk me over."

"Mmmm. Maybe I should."

"Sheila, come here, girl! Let me talk to you outside for a minute." Sheila and Renee went outside the room to talk.

"Sheila, I think you are moving way too fast. Are you sure this is something you want do?"

"Yes, girl! Everything keeps tingling. I want him so badly!"

"Sheila, you just met him. You don't even know him."

"I don't care. I'm tired of being a virgin. I want to know what it feels like. I'm tired of my pussy throbbing uncontrollably every time I see a fine nigga, and I want to give it to him, Renee. He already knows I'm a virgin and won't be expecting me to know what I'm doing anyway."

"Yeah, that's what I'm scared of. I don't want him to take something so precious from you and then give you his ass to kiss later. Are you prepared for that, too?"

"I wish he would, I'll kick that nigga's ass! I'm okay."

"Alright. Just want to make sure you know what you're getting yourself into. Love you, sis."

"Love you, too!" They hugged.

"I know he's the one, Renee. I can feel it."

Mission Impossible

They arrived at Thaddeus' dorm room. As Sheila and Thaddeus walked into the room, Sheila looked around.

"Which one is your bed? The top or bottom?"

"Bottom." Sheila sat on the bed and lay back on it.

"Come here," she said.

"Sheila, I need you to make sure you are ready for this?" Sheila started to kiss him.

"I'm ready."

"Are you sure you're a virgin?"

"Yes, and I just know what I want, so stop asking."

"I've just never seen or heard of a virgin this ready before."

"So, you've slept with a virgin before?"

"Yes. My ex was."

"How long did you stay with her after you two first did it?"

"2 years."

"You guys had to be in high school then."

"We dated for 3 years altogether. She became my girl in 10th grade, and we had sex for the first time later that summer."

"Was it your first time as well?"

"No, I used to fuck my babysitter."

"What?!" Sheila was startled.

"Yeah, she was a freak. She taught me a lot of shit."

"How old was she?"

"She was 17, and we fucked for about 3 years."

"Well, how old were you?"

"I was 13, until like 15 or 16."

"Damn, that's crazy!" Sheila shook her head in disbelief.

"Well, this means you were cheating on your girlfriend with your child-molesting ass babysitter."

"Damn, why she gotta be a child molester?"

"Because she is!"

"Well, I didn't look at it like that."

"Why not?"

"It was more like a learning lesson, like sex school—no feelings involved—just fucking and learning." Sheila shook her head in disbelief.

"Fuck that! I ain't never trusting babysitters when I have kids." Thaddeus laughed.

"If we have a son, it's cool, but if we have a little girl—fuck that!"

"Oh, I see! There's a double standard with you?"

"No. Little girls are different. They should be respected. They should take their time and do things on their terms. The decision should be solely up to them when it comes down to being sexual. It's a no brainer for men—we're dumb as shit. We just want it, hunt it, and destroy it. It's in our nature."

"Boy, shut up and kiss me. I want you to show me what your child molesting ass babysitter taught you." Thaddeus smiled, shaking his head

"You sure?"

"I'm positive. I knew I wanted you when I first laid eyes on you, and like you said, why wait to get to know each other when we're gonna do it anyway. Even 10 years from now, right?" Thaddeus looked at Sheila with a sexy but serious look. He pulled her by her ponytail, pulling her head back. Sheila got confused by the way he pulled her hair.

"Hold up! Now, wait a damn minute! Is it supposed to be this rough?"

"You said you want it, right?"

"Yeah, but I thought we were talking about having sex. The way you just pulled my hair, I thought we were about to fight."

"Sheila, didn't you tell me to shut up and kiss you?"

"Yes."

"Well, shut up and kiss me. I'll take the lead from here." Thaddeus pulled her ponytail again to tilt her hair back and put his tongue in her mouth. He kissed her and then whispered in her ear.

"Alright, I'm gonna give you this dick, but I need to warn you…"

"Warn me about what?" Sheila looked confused with panic.

"I don't have just any ol' average or little dick. I used to have my babysitter screaming, so I gotta make sure that pussy is nice and wet first because I don't wanna hurt you." Sheila got jealous thinking about him fucking his babysitter.

"Did you eventually fall in love with her?"

29

"I don't know. All I know is, I really loved fucking her."

"What about your ex? Did you love her?"

"Yes. I loved Jennifer." Sheila pushed him away.

"So, what happened? Why did you break up?"

"She didn't want to be in a long-distance relationship. She goes to school all the way out in Cali."

"Oh. Do you think you can love again?"

"I think I could love you, if you allow me to." He began to kiss Sheila on her neck. Sheila was loving the way he is making her feel, so she let out a deep breath and a soft moan.

"Mmmm. That feels so good. I hope it gets wet enough, so it doesn't hurt."

"Oh, I'm gonna make it wet." Thaddeus kissed her gently on the lips, penetrating his tongue in her mouth, rubbing her breasts as he slowly kissed down to her neck. He gently made his way down to her stomach and went up her shirt, kissing her bare skin. Sheila started to breathe heavily, as he got close to her nipples. Thaddeus started rubbing her nipples and kissing around her areola. He could feel her anticipation of him, wanting him to put it in his mouth. He teased her and made her wait for it. When he finally did, Sheila moaned and whispered.

"Oh, that shit feels so good."

Thaddeus whispered back.

"Oh, you like that shit, huh?" Thaddeus started to make his way back down her bare stomach, kissing her brown beautiful skin. He grabbed the sides of her sweatpants and pulled them down. With her help, he took off her panties as well. Thaddeus gently pushed her back to lay down, then opened her legs. He kissed up her thighs slowly, and her legs started to tremble. Then, he placed his lips on Sheila's clitoris and proceeded to gently suck and lick, suck and lick. Sheila gave off a medium to soft scream.

"Oh my God! What are you doing to me?!" The door opened.

"Oh shit! Sorry man, didn't know you had company." Thaddeus' roommate stood with a smile, Kay Kay standing next to him.

"What the fuck this bitch doing here?" Sheila jumped up, grabbing the sheets and her clothes to cover up.

"Yo! Thaddeus, you better handle your chick before Kay Kay fucks her up again!"

"What?! Fuck who up? Kay Kay don't want no more of this! She knows how I get down! That's why her face all fucked up!"

"Yeah, that's because you and your girl jumped her!" Dwight replied.

"What?! She and her girl jumped me. I whooped both of those bitches' asses!"

"Ain't that right, Kay Kay?!" Kay Kay turned away.

"Yeah, that's what the fuck I thought!" Sheila took a deep breath and swallowed real hard.

"Let me get dressed and get the fuck out of here, before I beat her ass again for lying to you like that!" Sheila yelled.

"Get the fuck out, so I can put my clothes on!" Thaddeus tried to calm Sheila.

"C'mon, Baby, you don't have to leave. This my room, too." Thaddeus plead, as Sheila ignored him getting dressed. Sheila pushed him to the side and stormed out the door. Thaddeus ran out right behind her.

Mission Complete

Back in Sheila and Renee's dorm, Renee and Jim were lying down watching, "The Godfather" when Sheila stormed in with Thaddeus right behind her. Renee jumps up!

"Damn, that was fast! What happened?!"

"Kay Kay's ass came in with Dwight!"

"Kay Kay?!"

"Yeah, girl! Right when Thaddeus was…" Sheila looked at Thaddeus and stopped herself from saying too much.

"Um…nevermind, but that Kay Kay bitch is a fucking liar! She told Dwight that you and I jumped her!"

"Oh, no that bitch didn't!" Thaddeus intervened, a little irritated.

"But you set it straight, and now they know the truth. So, why are you still mad?"

"You damn right I did!" She and Renee clapped high five with one another. Thaddeus shook his head, disappointed in the way they were bragging.

"Sheila, Baby, listen. You're too pretty to be letting some ghetto ass chick take you out of character like this. I don't condone women fighting, especially my woman. That shit ain't cute! I can't speak for anyone else, but it's not for me. I'm not having my girl out here fighting, fuck that!" Sheila humbled herself and got face-to-face with Thaddeus.

"Oh, I'm your woman?"

"I really would like you to be…"

"How soon?"

"I told you, we can do this shit now. Why wait to do what we are doing already. At least you can do what you want for the first time with your man and not some one-night stand. I want to get to know you and make sure everything you have to offer is not taken advantage of. I want everything about you to be cherished."

"Well, let's do it then."

"Alright, let's do it, but you gotta chill out with all that fighting and shit."

"Thaddeus, I'm not the one who started with them. I was only protecting myself. Sometimes, you've gotta prove yourself to these bitches—

that you're not to be fucked with."

"You don't have to prove yourself to no one. Alright?"

Sheila looked him in the eyes and didn't say a word. She gave him her undivided attention.

"So, now that you 'so called' proved yourself, you're done right?"

"Yes, I'm done, but…" Thaddeus cut her off.

"C'mon Sheila, you either done or you not?"

"I'm done."

"Okay, babe. That's what I want to hear. I'll see you tomorrow."

"What, you're leaving me?"

"Yeah, I need to take a cold shower—if you know what I mean!" Sheila laughed.

"Okay, okay. Go. I'll take care of that for you tomorrow." Sheila walked him to the door and gave him a long kiss goodnight. Jim got up and started putting on his shoes.

"Wait up, Thad. I'll walk back over with you." Jim tried to kiss Renee on the lips, but Renee mugged him and pulled away.

"Get your ass off me."

"Oh, I can't get a kiss?" Renee looked at him, rolled her eyes, and stuck out her cheek. Jim shook his head and kissed her cheek.

"Oh, I guess it's too much for me to ask, huh? I could've sworn I was just 'Husband' earlier, but that's alright. I'll wait. Can you at least walk me to the door?" Renee didn't move.

"Boy, if you don't walk your grown ass to the door."

Jim shook his head and proceeded to leave out the door.

"Bye, Jim. See you tomorrow." Jim's face lit up.

"Oh, is that an invitation?"

"Take it how you want."

"Invitation it is! I'll see you tomorrow, with your beautiful, evil ass." Renee laughed.

"Ain't nobody evil."

"That's alright. You don't know who you're messing with because, unlike other men, I love it! I love the chase! You turn me on every time your ass gets smart with me."

"Whatever, Jim. Bye!" They both laughed as he closed the door. Renee quickly turned and looked at Sheila, as soon as the door closed.

"So, did you do it?" she asked.

"Awww, damn, damn, damn….no!" Sheila kicked around in disappointment, as if she was kicking something other than air.

"What happened?"

"Girl, he was kissing all over my body, and the shit was feeling so fuckin' good! My lips, my neck, my stomach…then he slowly pulled down my pants and started sucking my pussy…"

"What?!"

"Yes, girl! That feeling was so fuckin' amazing! It was unbelievable!"

"Ooooh shit, girl! I've never gotten my pussy ate like that before."

"Shut up, Renee, before you spoil the moment because you never told me you got your pussy ate at all." Sheila gave an angry yet serious look to Renee.

"I swear to God, Sheila, I didn't! Mike only fucked me." Sheila rolled her eyes and continued on.

"Anyway, liar…as I was saying, it was fuckin' amazing! My legs were shaking uncontrollably, and I couldn't do a damn thing to control them either. It was crazy!"

"So, you did all that and didn't fuck?"

"Nope…because Kay Kay's ass walked in!"

"What?! What fuck was she doing there? Did she catch you in the act?"

"Yes, girl, pants down and all! I was so embarrassed, and I wanted to beat her ass so bad."

"Oh, damn!"

"Oh, damn is right! I was going crazy out of my mind because that shit felt so good. Girl, all I wanted to do was scream!" Sheila screamed and just stood there with this dumb ass smirk on her face.

"Oh my GOD! What did you do?"

"First, I had to set the record straight about who kicked whose ass, then I hurried up and put my clothes on and left. Girl, I was so embarrassed."

"Just imagine if you were sucking his dick?"

"Eww, I'm not sucking no dick!"

"What's wrong with sucking dick?"

"Oh, you suckin' dick now too, Renee. Then, got the nerve to be drinking out of my pop? I guess you forgot to tell me that shit, too?"

"Sorry." Renee put her head down.

"Wow, some kinda fuckin' friend you are."

"Sheila, let me be honest with you…"

"Oh, now you wanna be honest?" Sheila put her hand on her hips with an attitude.

"Sheila, you always talking about everybody—what they do in bed, how nasty they are and stuff…I didn't want to hear your mouth, so I kept it to myself."

"Whatever, Renee…you really thought I would talk about you?" Renee raised her eyebrows and shrugged her shoulders.

"I don't know."

"Really, Renee? I thought we were girls. You know you're like the sister to me. I would never do that to you."

"I'm sorry, Sheila. I wanted to tell you everything so bad. It was killing me. From this point forward, I will never keep anything from you, ever again." Renee held up her right hand.

"Cross your fingers, hope to die?" asked Sheila.

"Cross my fingers, hope to die." They both giggled.

"Well…what did you do to Thaddeus? Did you lick him at least?"

"No… I didn't know what to do."

"Oh my God, girl. They like to be touched, kissed on, and shit. Did you rub his dick?"

"No, I didn't touch him."

"So, you don't even know if he got a big one or a little one?"

"No."

"Girl, you've gotta size them up. You're supposed to always do a dick check."

"Why? Is that what you do?"

"Yes, girl. Nobody wants to waste their time with no little ding-a-ling." Renee laughed.

"You need to tell me something?"

"Oh, no." Sheila looked at Renee, her lips poked out and slightly twisted.

"Yeah okay, anyway. I didn't feel him down there, but he did warn me about how big it was."

"That's what they all say, but if it is, I feel for you, girl!" They both laugh.

"Girl, let me show you what to do, so you won't be stuck on stupid the next time."

"Show me?" Sheila looked confused.

"Yeah, nothing like that girl, I'm your sister. Now, after you kiss his lips, slowly move up to his kiss cheek, to his ear, and down his neck…" Renee started to slowly demonstrate on Sheila.

"Okay, as you slowly kiss him down his neck…" Sheila was still confused, as she repeated what Renee had just said.
"Take your hand and start rubbing his curly hair at the same time, while kissing his neck."

"Okay, girrrrrl…stop. Whew! That shit feels good." Renee laughed.

"It's supposed to feel good, silly! That's the point. This is how he's going to feel. Now, keep kissing him slowly…all the way down to his chest. Now take off your shirt."

"Huh?!"

"C'mon, take your shirt off, Sheila…let me show you how to play with his nipples."

"Oh, hell no!" Sheila laughed as she clinched her shirt.

"C'mon, Sheila. Don't you wanna be prepared for him the next time?"

"Yeah, but damn bitch, shit!"

"Bitch, shit what?" Renee asked with a little smile.

"That shit feels good…"

"I know. That's why I'm showing you. This is how you want him to feel the next time. C'mon, lift your arms up and take your shirt off."

"Oh my God, Renee...I don't know about this?" Sheila was scared and excited at the same time.

"Sheila, c'mon...trust me, girl. You wanna get Thaddeus' ass whipped or not?" Sheila complied with the exciting thought of whipping Thaddeus.

Renee started to take Sheila's shirt off. Sheila's voice went up an octave.

"What the fuck is going on?!" Sheila was confused, blushing and giggling all at the same time as Renee continued on.

"Now, lay back. When you get down to the nipples, don't go right at it. Kiss around it to tease him a little bit."

"It sounds like you fucked more than one time, bitch."

"No, it was only once...but I can tease my ass off. I'm what you call the BBQ," Renee laughed.

"What the hell is a BBQ, besides ribs, hamburgers, and hotdogs?"

"I'm the Blue Balls Queen." As they both laughed, Renee caught Sheila off guard by suddenly latching on to her nipple.

"Oh shit, got damn!" Sheila instantly stopped laughing and started to breathe heavily.

"Something just gushed out my pussy!"
Renee switched over to the other nipple, opening her mouth as she sucked it with a firm but gentle suck. Sheila grabbed Renee from the back of her head and pulled her into her chest even more. Sheila moaned and pulled Renee's hair. Renee continued on, as she felt the passion of Sheila's pull. Then, she looked up at her and kissed her. Sheila resisted and turned her head. Renee gently grabbed Sheila by her cheeks and turned her face around to kiss her again. Sheila eventually gave in and kissed her back. Renee took Sheila's hand and guided it to her breast, gently placing her hand on top of hers and easing her fingertips down, moving them in a circular motion to show her how to arouse her nipples. Renee took off her shirt, and Sheila did exactly what Renee told her to do. She teased the nipple, gently kissing around the areola and firmly but softly sucked it. Renee let off a moan, and guided Sheila's hand between her thighs to rub her pussy. Renee then put her hand down Sheila's sweats to feel her pussy. Sheila opened her legs to give Renee full access to feel her wetness.

"Mmmmm....you are so wet."
Sheila started to breathe even harder, moaning louder and breathing heavier. Renee started to kiss Sheila's navel, softly kissing and circling her tongue all the way down stopping at the line of her pubic area. She then looked up and whispered softly to Sheila...

"Can I taste your wet pussy?"

Sheila didn't respond. Even though she's felt amazing, she was confused about what was happening and how Renee knew all the amazing things she was doing. Renee was impatient. Without waiting for an answer, she started to pull down Sheila's sweats and continued to make her way, slowly kissing as she pulled her way down to Sheila's feet, removing her pants. Sheila's legs began to tremble as Renee licked and sucked her way back up. Sheila closed her legs quickly.

"No, Renee...we can't." Renee ignored Sheila's request. She reopened her legs and continued to kiss her inner thighs, rolling her tongue in a circular motion, moving closer and closer to Sheila's pussy.

"You sure you want me to stop?" Sheila didn't answer, so Renee continued teasing and kissing around Sheila's pussy. Sheila grabbed Renee by the back of her head and directed her straight to her pussy. Renee opened her mouth and latched onto Sheila's clitoris, sucking and gently wiggling her tongue.

"Oh shit! You feel so fuckin good, Renee!"

Then, there was a knock at the door! They both quickly snapped out of it, jumped up and looked at each other with embarrassment.

"Oh shit, was I loud?"

"I don't know..."

There was another knock. Renee yelled.

"Who is it?"

"Thaddeus!"

"One second, I'm changing into my pajamas," yelled Renee.

"What is he doing here?" They both put on their nightgowns. Renee jumped into bed and puled the covers over her. Sheila opened the door acting sleepy.

"Hey, Thaddeus...what's up?"

"I came to apologize..."

"Apologize for what?"

"For being so hard on you earlier, with that whole Kay Kay shit. It's not like you started it. You were only trying to protect yourself. I'm sorry for making you feel like you didn't have any rights to protect yourself." Sheila grinned from ear-to-ear and blushed.

"Thank you." Sheila kissed him on the lips to show her gratitude.

"Do you wanna come in, or is that it?" Thaddeus perked up and smiled.

"I'm coming in." Sheila turned off the lights and took him over to the bed. Thaddeus picked up the remote control, sat down, and started changing channels. Sheila fluffed her pillows and guided him to lay back as she played in his jet-black, curly, high top fade. Sheila whispered in his ear.

"I'm so glad you're here."

"Is that right?"

"Yes." Thaddeus raised an eyebrow.

"Why is that?" Sheila put her leg in between his and began to kiss him.

"I'm so horny."

"You're a virgin. What do you know about being horny?"

"Just because I'm a virgin, doesn't mean my pussy doesn't get wet and excited. My pussy is more excited now than it's ever been, so what are you going to do about it?"

"Where did you learn to talk like that? That's some real grown up shit."

"I'm just telling you how I feel…"

"You learned that shit watching pornos, didn't you?"

"No! Will you stop talking and fuck me?"

"Girl, I don't know where the hell you are getting this from, but it's turning me the fuck on." He grabbed her hand and rubbed his dick with it. You feel that? You got my dick harder than Chinese arithmetic right now." Sheila felt the thickness and the long width of his hard dick.

"No girl has ever talked dirty to me like that but my babysitter, and that shit drives me crazy! You sure you want all of this big dick?"

"I said fuck me, didn't I?" She took off her clothes, leaving on her bra and panties, and lay back on the bed.
Thaddeus got up and took off everything but his boxers. He lay on top of Sheila, pulling the covers over them.

"What about Renee?"

"If I'm not concerned about her, why should you be?" Thaddeus, not thinking twice about it, proceeded to grind his dick on her pussy, kissing her lips as he rubbed her breast. Sheila started to moan.

"On my God, Thaddeus! Your dick feels so good rubbing on my pussy. Take off your boxers." As she felt penetration from his grind at the entry of her vagina, anxiously, she grinds harder, grabbing and pulling him in by his ass.

"I want you to put it in, now." She grinds harder.

"I'm so fucking horny!"

"I need to take my time with you. I don't want to hurt you. Let me kiss it and get it nice and wet."

"It's already wet." Sheila flipped him over and started pulling down his boxers. Thaddeus was confused.

"What the fuck is going on? I thought you were a virgin?"

"I am." She kissed down his neck, down his chest, and slowly kissed around his nipples. Then, she gently latched on with a suck, just like Renee had taught her, moving her tongue in a circular motion.

"Damn, girl! Suck that shit." Sheila got on top of him in a squatting position, took his dick and rubbed it between her pussy. She got it right at the entry of her pussy and tried to push it in…

"Oh my God, it's not going in." Thaddeus flipped her onto her back and started to whisper in her ear. Thaddeus started kissing and licking her and went down to give her oral.

"That shit feels so good. My pussy is throbbing so bad. I'm ready. I want you to try to put it in me again." Thaddeus got real excited.

"You want this dick? Okay, I'm going to give you this dick." He started to gently penetrate little-by-little, and more and more, penetrating faster and faster. Sheila moaned and breathed heavily.

"Yes, baby just like that. I want this dick so bad."
Thaddeus' strokes got more intense, and his moans got louder. Sheila was feeling his dick in her pussy.

"Oh my God!" She yelled loudly and passionately. She let out a loud moan.

"It hurts…" Thaddeus continued to stroke her pussy, but then he suddenly paused, took a deep breath, and swallowed as he felt his heart beating in his chest.

"You want me to stop?"

"No, I can take it."

"Damn, I love this tight pussy, right here."
As her pussy started to open, his strokes became faster and deeper. Sheila

moaned louder and cried out. Meanwhile, Renee was peeking and watching the whole thing. As they continued to make love and build chemistry, Thaddeus' moans turned into grunts.

"Oh, shit! I'm about to cum!" He fucked her harder, deeper, and faster; the more Sheila screamed, the harder he fucked her. Thaddeus let out a sign of exhaustion and lay all his sweaty, dead weight on top of Sheila. He then kissed her on the lips, as he rolled off her.

"Are you okay?" he asked, as they both lay there breathing hard.

"Oh my God, yes!" Sheila replied with a smile, kissing him back. Renee pulled the covers over her head and pretended to be asleep.

Homecoming

"F-I-G-H-T Fight Wildcats fight!" Sheila cheers with Renee, as Renee cheers from the field for their school football team. Sheila and Thaddeus are sitting in the front row, visible to Renee. Sheila is chanting the cheers with the cheerleaders, along with a few other people in the stands.

"Go Wildcats!" Sheila yelled, waving the pom-poms she got from the pep rally earlier. Renee waved at some of her friends, Tamika and Kelly. They were just getting to the game and sat behind Sheila and Thaddeus.

"Hey, Sheila!"

"Oh hey, Tamika! Hey, Kelly! A friend with them spoke to Thaddeus."

"Hey, Thad." Thaddeus turned around and spoke back.

"What's up Gee Gee?" Sheila turned around to get a better look at Gee Gee. Gee Gee whispered to Tamika and Kelly.

"Damn, what? I can't speak? Nobody wants her fuckin' man."

"You better chill with that shit. That's my fuckin girl, and trust me, you don't want none of that—Sheila will fuck your ass up" Tamika warned. Gee Gee frowned her face and folded her arms.

"So, what are you saying?" Kelly leaned over to intervene and whispered to Gee Gee as well.

"She is saying, Sheila is going to whoop your ass if you keep fuckin' with her, and we are not fuckin' helping you."

"Why it gotta be all like that? I only spoke to his ass...damn!" Kelly looked at her, shaking her head.

"Okay, Bitch, learn the hard way!" Sheila pretended as if she couldn't hear the conversation.

"C'mon, Wildcats!" Sheila and Thaddeus yelled. "C'mon, Jim! Stop these mutha'fuckas! Gee Gee repeats what Thaddeus just yelled.

"Yeah, c'mon Jim! Stop these mutha'fuckas!" Gee Gee looked over at Thaddeus. Sheila was not missing a beat from her peripheral but continued watching the game.

"Awww!" Everyone sighed because the long pass thrown from the visiting team just put them in field goal range.

"Come the fuck on, man! Sack that mutha'fucka! He's always open, damn!" Thaddeus yelled.

"Come the fuck on, man! Sack that mutha'fucka, he's always open... damn! Gee yelled, mocking Thaddeus.

Gee Gee looked at Thaddeus again and smiled. Kelly and Tamika shook their heads. Thaddeus turned around and smiled back at Gee Gee.

Sheila, with her lips very tight, said, "If you turn your ass around again and look at that bitch one more time, I'm gonna fuck your ass up!"

"C'mon, Sheila! We're having fun. You better go somewhere with that shit, and stop getting all jealous." He put his arms around her neck and kissed her on the cheek, trying to soften the mood.

"C'mon, Baby, cross your fingers and pray they'll miss this field goal."

"With six seconds left 'til halftime, if the Panthers make it, they will take the lead," the announcer yells.

"...and the field goal is good!" Everyone sighed, getting up from their seats. Renee and the cheerleaders cheered.

"That's alright, that's okay, we're gonna beat you anyway! That's alright, that's okay, 're gonna beat you anyway! Yaaayyy!" Renee yelled at Sheila.

"Wait right there. I'll be right up!"

"Okay! Sheila turned around to Thaddeus and asked, "Did you used to go with her?"

"No."

"Well, why the bitch was all on your jock like that and shit?! What's that all about?" Thaddeus laughed.

"You need to cut that jealous shit out, Sheila. Sheila swung at him in a playful way, and Thaddeus leaned back for the miss. Renee walked up, having overheard.

"Who's jealous?"

"Your girl."

"No, I'm not, Renee. I just think that bitch was trying to be smart. Fuckin' floozy!"

"Who?"

"Some Gee Gee bitch. She was with Tamika and Kelly."

"Oh, that bitch!?"

"You know her?"

"Yeah, she was all up in Jim's face last week."

"Word!?"

"Yeah, he said she's a fuckin' whore and nobody wants her stank ass. He said she be fuckin' niggas all in the locker room and shit."

"Hmmm…that shit sounds familiar."

"Oh, bitch, you tryna be smart?!" Sheila laughed, as Thaddeus intervened.

"This sounds a little too personal for me. I'm gonna catch up with the fellas." He gave Sheila a peck on the lips.

"I'll meet you back here, Baby. Thaddeus started up the steps as Sheila and Renee followed. Renee quickly stopped.

"Girl, did I tell you the Panthers' quarterback is in love with you?"

"What? How does he even know me?" She blushed.

"Jim showed him a picture of us, and apparently, he loves a phat ass. Jim said he was going crazy over your picture."

"What does he look like?"

"He's fine as shit!"

"I can't see his face with that helmet on."

"That's okay. I'll introduce you two after the game."

"No, girl! I'm with Thaddeus!"

"Well, he won't know why I'm introducing you two. I'll introduce his ass to him, too." They both laughed!

"Girl, you are a mess.'"

"And, girl, you've got a lot to learn." Renee shook her head. "When I do introduce you, don't get all paranoid and shit. Just stay calm, and act like you never heard of him."

"Alright, girl." They proceeded to mingle with friends.

Three minutes into the third quarter of the game, Sheila sat down looking for Thaddeus. She saw Tamika and Kelly behind her but no Gee Gee. Sheila instantly started to get bad thoughts in her head. She crossed her arms, twisted her lips, and shook her leg, as she kept looking back at the steps. She contemplated going out there to find his ass. Then, Sheila got up and said excuse me to the people sitting next to her. After moving through the aisle, she looked up and saw Thaddeus making his way down the steps. She shook her head and threw her hands up, telling people nevermind and sorry, and as she made her way back to her seat. Thaddeus made his way through the people as well and noticed a nonchalant look on Sheila's face.

"What's wrong, Baby?"

"Nothing. C'mon on, Wildcats!"

Sheila yelled and then noticed Gee Gee making her way through to her seat as well. Sheila turned around and pointed her finger in Thaddeus' face.

"   Where the fuck was you?"

"Damn! Where the fuck did that come from?"

"Don't fucking play with me, Thaddeus!"

"I was waiting for my sandwich," he replied, holding the sandwich up in Sheila's face.

"Yeah, whatever." Thaddeus shook his head, opened the wrapping on his sandwich, and took a bite. Then, he held it up to Sheila.

"You want a bite?" Sheila opened her mouth and extended her neck over to take a bite.

"Mmmm…that's good! What's that?"

"Hot roast beef with provolone cheese."

"Mmmm…you've gotta get me one next time."

"Yeah, that gravy is the shit, isn't it?"

"Yes, but this was pre-cooked. Why the hell it take so long to get back to your seat?"

"It was a long line. Why you keep questioning me?"

"Because I can, that's why!" He gave Sheila another bite.

"Mmmm…oh my God, this sandwich is the bomb! Thanks for the heads up on the sandwich, Thad! It's sooo good!" Gee Gee interrupted. Sheila quickly got up and leapt over the seat, pushed Kelly outta the way, and punched Gee Gee in the face. Everyone jumped up! Thaddeus grabbed Sheila off of Gee Gee.

"What the fuck you do that for, Sheila?!"

"That bitch kept pushing my fuckin buttons, and you know it!"

"She didn't even do anything to you!" Tamika and Kelly held Gee Gee back.

"Let me go! That bitch fucking snuck me! Let me the fuck go!" Tamika told her to calm down and kept trying to pull her away.

"You had that shit coming, Bitch! When you keep fucking with me, shit like this happens!"

"Nobody was fucking with you, you insecure bitch! I don't want Thaddeus' ass. I had him before, and if I wanted his ass again, he would be right here sniffing this ass again, you psycho bitch! I've been there, done that!" Sheila broke away from Thaddeus and leapt over the bench again to fight Gee Gee. Tamika and Kelly let go of Gee Gee to prevent any controversy regarding their friendship with the two. Renee ran up from the field yelling.

"Get the fuck off her!"

Thaddeus tried to pull Sheila off of Gee Gee, while Tamika and Kelly were helping Gee Gee off the ground and between the seats. Thaddeus had a hold on Sheila and pulled her away from the scene.

"What the fuck happened, Tamika?!" asked Renee.

"Girl! Long story, but trust me, Sheila is cool. She's just upset right now."

Renee ran out to catch up with Sheila and Thaddeus. She found them in the parking lot, arguing.

"What the fuck happened, Sheila?!"

"I'm done. Take your girl to your room!" Thaddeus yelled, walking away.

"Where the hell are you going?" Renee yelled.

"Leave him alone, Renee. He's probably going to check on that bitch!" Sheila yelled it loud enough for Thaddeus to hear. Thaddeus turned around and gave her the finger.

"Yeah, fuck you, too!" Thaddeus kept walking.

"Sheila! What the hell happened?"

Sheila started telling the story fast and upset.

"First, the bitch comes in all cute and sassy with her 'Hi, Thaddeus' shit. Then, she thought I didn't hear what she was saying to Tamika and Kelly, talking about, 'What? I can't speak to him?" Sheila was making all these hand gestures and rolling her neck, while she told the story.

"Then, she kept trying to be smart by mocking Thaddeus' every word to get his attention. Then, to top it all off, they both came back to their seats all

late at the same fucking time, which she wanted me to know about by saying, 'Thanks for the heads up, Thad. This sandwich is sooo good!"
Sheila imitated the way Gee Gee spoke.

"Oh, that bitch deserved that beat down! I would've done the same thing!"

"Yeah, like your ass can fight!"

"I can get the job done, that's all that matters."

"Oh, girl, stop being so damn sensitive." Sheila stopped and yelled.

"Oh my GOD!" she screamed, holding her hands to her head while starting to cry.

"What?!" Renee instantly hugged her.

"That mutha'fucka is a liar! He told me he never fucked that bitch! He allowed her to play me like a fool!"

"How?! What do you mean?"

"When they pulled me off her, she said I was jealous because she had him before me, and if she wanted him again, she could have him!"

"Get the fuck out of here!?"

"Yes, that's why I'm so mad and upset right now!"

"Well, let's go in and chill out, so we can get our minds right for the party tonight."

"I'm not thinking about no fuckin' party! I'm not going!"

"Why not, Sheila?!"

"I don't know how to feel right now, Renee."

"C'mon, Sheila. It will help take things off your mind. Besides, I don't want to go without you."

"I don't want to see him Renee, and I know he's going to be there. I'm mad at the fact that he's not even here with me now, making sure I'm cool. This shit is driving me crazy! Do you think he's with her?"

"I don't know, Sheila…maybe, maybe not. Don't jump to conclusions."

"Ugh! I need to know."

"No, Sheila! C'mon, let's just chill. You're just a little strung out over your first."

"Well, I don't remember you being all crazy over Mike like this. I guess that's why I never knew you two even did anything. There were no signs."

"That's because he left my ass right after I gave him some."

"What?! Oh damn, Renee."

"Yeah, girl! He acted like he didn't even know me. I was all excited about seeing him the next day. Girl, there was no eye contact or anything. He just gave me a sorry ass wave and walked by my ass, like he didn't even know me."

"Girl, I would've kicked Thaddeus' ass if he would've pulled that shit on me!"

Sheila put her arm around Renee as they walked.

"Damn, sorry friend. It's a shame your first turned out to be that way. If you would've told me, I could've been there for you."

"Thanks, sis! I'm over it though." Sheila hugged her again.

"Well, I have to make another confession…"

Sheila stopped and looked at her.

"Mike actually wasn't my first experience…my first experience was with a girl!" Renee took off running.

Sheila yelled, "You know what, Renee, you're a fuckin' liar, just like that damn Thaddeus!" Renee kept running and laughing.

"You know I run track, so if I wanted to catch your slow ass I could!" Sheila finally caught up with Renee. When she walked into the room, Renee was under the covers with a pillow on her face. Sheila snatched off the covers and pillow and pointed a finger in her face.

"You know what you have too many damn secrets, bitch, to be considering yourself to be my best friend!"

"I'm sorry, Sheila. I had to keep that one from you."

"Why, Renee?"

"Because I didn't want you to judge me since I'm Bi. I didn't want you to start acting all funny towards me. Thinking I want you or something…"

"You did. You made that quite clear a few months ago." Renee turned her head with a smirk on the face.

"So, when I was getting undressed in front of your ass, you were looking at my titties, ass, and shit?"

"See! This is what I didn't want to happen, Sheila! Look at you, judgin' me. It wasn't even like that, Sheila."

They both got quiet and looked at each other.

Renee then burst out, "You do have some pretty ass titties though. I couldn't wait to put my mouth on them pretty ass nipples!" Renee started to laugh as Sheila blushed. Then, there was a knock at the door.

"Who is it?"

"Jim."

Renee got up to answer the door. Jim came in mad and upset.

"What the fuck happened at the game?"

"Sheila was fighting Gee Gee."

"Nobody touched you, right?"

"No."

"Good, I was worried. I thought I would have to fuck somebody up! Tasha gave me your bag with your stuff in it and said you were fighting."

"No, I left to make sure Sheila was okay."

"So, just fuck me huh, Jim?"

"Oh, shit! Sorry Sheila, nothing like that. I know Thad had your back. I needed to check on my baby. You and Thad were together, right?" Sheila flagged what Jim is saying.

"Don't tell me my man ain't have your back?"

"It was over him."

"What? Where is he?"

"Your guess is as good as mine."

"Well shit, on that note, let me bring my man in, if that's okay with you?"

"Who and where is he?"

"My man, Matt. He's waiting right outside the door. I didn't want to disrespect Thad, so I told him to wait outside."

Renee jumped up with a big smile.

"Matt! Sheila, that's the guy I was telling you about…the quarterback! Jim stepped out to get him."

Sheila whispered to Renee.

"What about Thaddeus?"

"What about him?" Jim walked back in.

"Sheila, this is Matt. Matt, this is Sheila."

51

"Oh, shit! He is white?! Renee, why you didn't warn me?"
Matt raised an eyebrow and gave Sheila a puzzling look.

"Warn you?" asked Jim. The mood got awkward.

"Oh, shit! Am I?! You mean to tell me, Jim, after all these years, you never told me my ass is white?"
Matt ran over to the mirror and looked at his face.

"She's a fucking genius!" he said sarcastically.

"Jim, you better tell your friend to leave me the fuck alone. I'm not in the mood for no dumb shit!"

"Well, Sheila…" Jim started, but Matt cut Jim off.

"No, Jim, let me take care of this…"

"I don't think you wanna do this man," Jim attempted.

"I think you were quite rude to me, Sheila. No 'Hi,' 'Hello,' or nothing. Instead, what did I have to hear? 'Oh, he's white!?' Talking about how someone should have warned you? What the fuck is that supposed to mean?!"
Sheila folded her arms and started to shake her leg.

"Ok, Buddy, I think she gets it."
Sheila interjects, "No, I'm not saying it like that Matt…"

"Hold up, wait one minute, um…excuse me, Sheila. I did warn you, remember?" Renee intervened.

"Babe, what you just said ain't help shit. You could've kept that shit to yourself." Jim shook his head.

"Wow, Renee! Just throw me under the bus. I'm done with this."

"Oh, I guess that's how you resolve issues, huh?" Matt asked. "I take it you just shut it down and run from them, huh?"

"Matt, I don't have to run from shit!"

"Well, you didn't resolve it either. Just take accountability for your actions. If you're wrong, just say you're wrong, apologize, or something."
Sheila cleared her throat as she folded her arms again and bit her bottom lip, looking downward at the floor.

"Okay, Matt. I'm sorry." She looked up at him. "Will you please accept my apology? That shit was out of line."

"Hell yeah, with your gorgeous ass…apology accepted!"

"Oh, shit! This is the first time anybody has shut her ass down. This may work…"

"Oh, shut up, Jim! Ain't nobody shut nobody the hell down. I was wrong. Besides, you know my situation, so you know I can't see no one right now."

"Excuse me for a second." Renee cut her off.

Renee grabbed Sheila by the arm, and pulled her aside, whispering.

"Just one second. Girl, fuck Thaddeus! His ass ain't thinking about you, so fuck him! Play this shit out until you know for sure where you and Thaddeus stand."

Renee looked back to see if they could hear her and then turned back around to Sheila as she rolled her eyes. Renee continued talking with tight lips, as she leaned in to speak again.

"Forreal, forreal, Bitch! You can play them both. Matt is across town at one school, and Thaddeus is at another—girl that's an easy fuckin' win!"

"No, that's too much. I can't date them both." Jim cleared his throat.

"Excuse me, ladies, but are y'all talking about us?"

"Yeah, we're talking about y'alls asses! Give me a minute!" Renee sucked her teeth and rolled her eyes.

"Girl, c'mon, I'll school your ass later. Just get his number for now." Renee pulled her back to the full circle.

"Well, I hope whatever you were talking about is good," asked Jim.

"You know, I only have nothing but good things to say about you, Baby. So, Matt, are you coming to the party tonight?"

"I don't know. Jim tryna talk me into going."

"Hell yeah, he's going! We got a dope ass show! LL Cool J, Schoolly D, Mantronix, Ultra Magnetic MCs, and Yvette Money—I'm hype as shit!"

"So, Matt, what you know about Hip Hop?"

"Excuse you! There you go again, Sheila. Would you have asked me these questions if I was Black?"

"No, I'm just trying to figure you out, that's all."

"Don't know much about White men, and since you're in a predominantly white college, I'm quite sure they're not playing Hip Hop over there."

"Why not? Do you always make these kinds of assumptions based on someone's race?"

"It was just a question. Forgive me, I'm learning."

"Okay, I'll give you a pass this time, but the next time..."

"The next time, what?" She folded her arms.

"Relax, I'm just joking, Sheila." Matt laughed.

"I must say, you're honest, and I like that." They both smiled. They play a little Hip Hop, R&B, pop and rock at my school.

"Can you dance?"

"Sheila, really? You don't know when to quit, do you?" Jim was frustrated.

"What? I can't ask questions?"

"Sure, you can, go ahead and ask all the questions you want. I'm an open book. What do you want to know?" asked Matt.

"I want to know if you can dance."

"I can slow dance, and if you promise me one, I'll show you." Sheila blushed with a smile.

"Oh, wait! Is that a fuckin' smile?" Everyone laughed

"Question, Sheila…where's your boyfriend?"

Renee quickly got behind Matt and signaled to her no.

"Um, I don't have a boyfriend."

"Awesome!"

"Awesome?" Sheila and Renee laughed.

"Oh…I see you guys are making fun of me."

"You guys?" Sheila quickly stopped herself from laughing.

"No, Matt. It's cool, just a little different for us, but it's cute." Matt smiled.

"Did you hear that, Jim? She said I'm cute."

"I did not say all of that."

"I'm not cute?"

Sheila ignored the question.

"I'll give you a dance, Matt."

"Well, I guess I'll see you there," he winked at Sheila.

"C'mon, man! Let's head back to my dorm, so we can get dressed. I'll see you later, Baby." Jim gave Renee a kiss before they walked out the door.

Sheila and Renee had a blast at Homecoming. Sheila tried to have fun but couldn't take her mind off of Thaddeus. She kept watching the door and wondering when he was going to walk in. Halfway through the party, Renee was able to get Sheila to relax and enjoy the rest of the night. She convinced her that he wasn't coming if he wasn't there by now. Jim, Renee, Sheila and Matt began to dance the rest of the night, having a ball. When the night ended, Jim and Matt walked the ladies to their room to say goodnight. Matt thanked Sheila for a wonderful night, as they exchanged numbers.

Sheila waited for a pop-up visit, hoping to get an apology from Thaddeus, but days, weeks, and months went by without a word from Thaddeus. Sheila began to occupy her time with school, talking to Matt every day on the phone, and seeing him on weekends. Even though they have grown closer in their friendship, Sheila remained reserved, as far as a relationship or taking what they have to another level.

Moving On

At 12:10 p.m. Sheila's head had been down for the majority of the time in class.
As the class cleared, Professor Jones goes over to Sheila and wakes her with a
shake on her shoulder.

"Sheila, Sheila..."
Her professor continued to shake her. Sheila looked up, squinting her eyes trying
to make sense of what was going on.

"Hey, you slept through my whole class. What's going on with you?
You haven't been yourself lately."

"I'm sorry, Professor Jones. I haven't been getting any sleep lately, but
I'll make sure I get some over the weekend."

"I hope so because you're starting this semester off on the wrong foot.
You're a mature and talented student, so whatever it is, I'm sure it's not worth
you compromising your GPA."

"No, it's not, Professor Jones. You will see a totally different me
showing up on Monday, I promise."

"All right, I'll see you bright and early on Monday, Sheila."

"Yes, you will! Thank you, Professor Jones." Sheila grabbed her things
and headed out of the classroom.

"Hey, Sheila! What's going on with you?"

"Hey, Eric."

"Why have you've been sleeping so much lately? You must pregnant or
something."

"Hell no! Are you crazy?"

"Naw. You know how it is when girls sleep all the time."

"Well, not me."

"Oh, I know what it is!" Sheila put her hand on her hip and looked at
him with raised eyebrows, waiting to hear what Eric had to say.
"Your little heart is still broken."

"No, it's not! You don't fuckin' know me, so stop acting like you do!"
Sheila walked off with an attitude.

"Well, damn, Sheila! Why it gotta be like that? You all cursing at me
and being so defensive. I'm just trying to help."

"No, you're not. You're being nosey."

"Well, maybe I am. I need to know you're over Thad, before I ask you out."

Sheila turned around laughing.

"What's so funny? I'm tryna talk to you, take you out, and you're laughing at me, as if I'm some kind of joke or something."

"Because I thought it was."

"Why is that? I'm not your type?"

"I'm not saying that, Eric. You never showed any interest before, so why now?"

"How can I show you I'm interested in you, with you being all in love with Thaddeus?"

"Thaddeus and I broke up long before summer break."

"Damn, it's been that long? Well, okay. Now that it's confirmed that you two are not together anymore, I can make all the moves I want."

"Cute, Eric." Sheila started laughing as she walked away.

"Oh, that's all I get...cute Eric?"

Sheila laughed and continued to walk out the door. Eric hurried to catch up with her.

"C'mon, Sheila! On a more serious note, let's go to the movies tonight."

"Oh, you really serious, Eric?"

"Yeah, why wouldn't I be? You're fine as hell. Who wouldn't be attracted to you?" Sheila blushed.

"Okay, Eric. We're on, but I get to pick the movie."

"I was going to ask you to choose anyway cause it's all about you."

"Is that right?"

"Absolutely! Here's my number," he said, handing her a piece of paper.

"Just let me know what movie you want to see, the time, and we out."

"Okay. I'll call you when I get back to the dorm." They both walked away from one another and headed to their dorms.

The phone was ringing when Sheila walked into her room. She hurried to catch it.

"Hello?"

"Hello, Gorgeous."

"Hi, Matt." She smiled at the realization of it being him on the other end of the line.

"What are you doing this weekend?"

"Nothing. Why? What's up?"

"Jim thought we should all hook up this weekend."

"Ummm…okay. Are you coming up tonight or tomorrow night?"

"I'll drive up tonight. The sooner I see you, the better." Sheila blushed.

"Oh, is that right?" Renee walked in.

"If I'm lying, I'm flying." Sheila laughed.

"Matt, you don't even talk like that."

"I know. I borrowed that line from Jim."

"Well, you need to give it back." They both laughed. "At least I got the reaction I was expecting. You're laughing, and I can see your beautiful smile all the way from here." Sheila smiled harder.

"Damn! Who's got your ass cheesing all on the phone?" asked Renee.

"I'm talking to Matt. He's coming up for the weekend."

"Oh, shit! Matt can't keep his ass away from you. He's been up here damn near every weekend, except for maybe two of them, and he even came over your house during break. Hmmmm…I know what it is! Matt is tryna get into those panties!" yelled Renee.

"Oh my God! No, you didn't, Renee!"

"Oh yes, the fuck I did! Somebody gotta say it. You two been beating around the bush too long. I mean, like literally." Renee laughed.

"   Y'all need to stop frontin' and make it happen."

"Sheila, don't listen to Renee. You know I would never rush you into making any big decisions like that. I want you to take your time. I enjoy spending time with you, and that's it."

"Awww, that's really sweet, Matt. Thank you."

"Awww, what did he say?"

"Nothing, Renee. Mind your business. This is between A and B, so C your way out of it."

"Oh, y'all need to stop frontin'. You know you're both glad I said it. Bet y'all will be fuckin' by the weekend."

Renee and Sheila laughed. Sheila held her hand over the phone, so Matt didn't hear.

"Matt, I'll see you when you get here, gotta go! This girl is in rare form right about now." Sheila hung up.

"Why you always starting something, Renee?' Sheila laughed.

"So, you're not tryna fuck Matt?"

"I don't know…he's cute, but…he's also White. I never pictured myself with a White man before. What would people say?"

"Fuck what people say! You want him, don't you?"

"I don't know."

"What you mean, you do know? You don't get all tingly inside, like you did with Thaddeus?"

"Yeah, I do."

"Well, what are you waiting for?"

"I don't know. I am a bit curious…and horny as hell." She laughed. "I haven't had any in a year."

"Well, go for it, sis! Do you!" Sheila cut Renee off.

"Oh shit, Eric!"

"Eric? Who the fuck is Eric?"

"He's in my Psychology class."

"Yeah, and? What about him?"

"He's taking me to the movies tonight."

"Okay, bitch!" She snapped her fingers, as if she was reading her mind.

"Thaddeus who?" They laughed and slapped high five.

"When did this happen?"

"Today, after class. He's said he's been on me for a minute, but he didn't want to approach me because he knew I was going with Thaddeus."

"Oh okay! A respectful nigga." Renee laughed. "Sounding all corny and shit!"

"C'mon, stop it, Renee. He's not corny. He's really cute. He's clean cut and laid back. He reminds me of that new sexy singer, Al B. Sure—but the chocolate version."

Renee cut her off.

"Oh, that man is fine then! You know I love me some Al B. Sure!

Sheila, I'm telling you...this mutha'fucka better look like him too, and you better not be pulling my leg."

"No... that's the shit you do, Renee." Sheila laughed. "What would I get out of lying to you?"

"I don't know, but I know if he is that fine, I' should've seen his ass somewhere on campus by now, after being here a year."

"I'm telling you; he is! Eric looks like Al B. Sure's twin, just chocolate. I just didn't think he was on me like that."

"Yeah, okay. If you say so."

"Meanwhile, Renee...what am I going to do with Matt?"

"Just go out with Eric. Play like you're a respectful type of chick, so you can get your ass back here early."

"Bitch, I am respectful!" Sheila hit Renee playfully and Renee laughed.

"I know, I know. It's just jokes girl, but you've gotta cut your night short. I'll tell Matt you're braiding Kelly's hair or something."

"Yeah, that sounds like a plan. Let me get on the phone now and find the earliest movie."

Eric walks Sheila to her room after their time at the movies.

"Thanks for hanging out with a brother. I had a great time."

"So did I."

"It's still early. Can I come in and talk?"

"No, not tonight. I really gotta catch up on some sleep. I am so tired."

"Yeah, you were knocked out in class today."

"Yeah, don't remind me. That was so embarrassing."

"Naw, don't be. Get your rest, and maybe we can catch up on things tomorrow."

"Okay, we'll see. I really need to refresh this whole weekend."

"Okay, I'm not going to push the issue. I just really like you and want to get to know you better, that's all."

Eric walked away but then turned around.

"Hold up, you never gave me your number."

"302-555-6982."

"6982, 6982, 6982."

Eric kept saying to himself as he walked away. Sheila waited until he walked down the stairway to open the door. As she walked in, Renee was sitting on the bed watching TV.

"Where are Matt and Jim?"

"They went to Hardee's to grab us some food. I told him to get you that burger you always get with a Pepsi."

"Whew! Oh, okay. That was a close call!"

"What was?"

"Eric just walked me to the door. What if they came up while Eric was out there?"

"Oh damn, I missed him?"

"Yeah, I had to get rid of him as fast as I could."

"I need to see what his corny ass looks like! We've got a rep to protect."

"I told you, he's not corny. He's about 6'1, chocolate complexion, pretty white teeth, dark curly hair, and he dresses really nice."

"Damn, his corny ass sounds fine as shit!"

"Please, can you stop it with the corny shit? He is the fuck fine."

"Oh, shit! You must really like him?"

"Yes, especially after tonight."

"Damn. Well what happened tonight?"

"Oh, nothing like that. He was just so attentive, and the way he spoke to me was so sexy. He was so calm and direct. Every time he talked to me, he looked me right in my eyes, and that shit had my pussy tingling."

"That's because you ain't had none since Thaddeus bust that cherry." They both laughed.

"How long have Jim and Matt been gone?"

"About a half hour. They should be on their way back."

"Not if it's crowed. You know how crowed Hardee's is on the weekends."

"So… did you decide if you giving Matt the panties?"

"I don't think so. We'll see what happens."

"I can't wait."

"Why the hell can't you wait?"

"Girl, I'm gonna live vicariously through you. I wanna know what it's like to fuck a white boy, and if the myth is true?"

"What's the myth?"

"That they got little dicks but know how to eat the shit out of some pussy."

"Is that right?"

"I don't know. That's only what I heard."

"So, what is Jim like in bed? You never talk about him."

"Oh, Jim can fuck his ass off. I know your ass be hearing us fucking, acting like you're sleep." They laughed.

"I know your horny ass wants to join us, don't you?"

"Ewww, no! You fuckin' freak!"

Sheila pushed her by her shoulder as they fell back and laughed. Sheila got back up.

"Yeah, I be hearing your ass screaming and shit, but you lie so much, I'm not sure if you're faking it or not."

"You see my freak ass hasn't been with no one else but Jim during this past year. Besides, Jim fucks me so much, he makes sure there's nothing left for no one else." They gave each other a high five and laughed.

"Girl, you talked all that shit and…"

A knock at the door cut them off from talking.

"Oh shit, that's them!" Sheila blushed.

"Who is it?!"

"Your husband!"

Renee got up to open the door, as Jim and Matt came in holding a Hardee's bag and carrying pops. Sheila got up to help Matt with the bag and kissed him. Matt instantly knew that kiss was different. It was more sensual.

"Hmmm. Hey, Gorgeous."

"Hey Matt." Sheila looked at him again and began to kiss him even longer and stronger, and she placed her tongue all in his mouth. Matt turned around and looked at Jim and Renee.

"Okay, take your meals to go, you guys have to leave!"

"Well, damn! Can we finish our food first, while it's hot?"

"Not if she keeps kissing me like this." Sheila blushed.

"C'mon, Matt. Let's eat, and I'll finish what I started later."

"Well, I hope I don't choke because I'm about to make this food disappear fast as hell." Sheila laughed.

"Boy, if you don't take your time! You know we have all weekend." They smiled at each other.

"C'mon, Babe…before his ass chokes to death. We can finish this on our way to your room."

"Yeah, I can clearly see that we are cock-blocking."
Jim and Renee shook their heads as they laughed and gathered their food. Sheila and Matt smiled as they flirted with each other on her bed.

"Alright man, I guess I'll be seeing tomorrow." They gave each other a handshake, as Jim and Renee exited the room.

"Whew, I thought they'd never leave!"

"Yeah, looks like it's just you and me." She got closer to him on the bed.

"Wait a minute, where did this whole desire for me begin?"

"I don't know."

"I don't know," Matt imitated her.

"Stop it, Matt. I don't know…I guess I really like you, and I've been scared to approach you because…"

"Because I'm White?" Sheila didn't say anything.

"It's okay, Sheila. This is new for me as well."

"I didn't want to offend you again, and we know I can be really good at that."

"Don't worry about offending me, Sheila. Be yourself. I love that fire and honesty in you. I must admit, it took me a minute to understand you, but once I had the chance to get to know you, it made me respect you more. I'd rather for you to speak your mind and be truthful, than to be gassing me up with lies." Sheila laughed.

"Oh, listen to you, 'Gassing me up.'

"Oh, White people say that, too."

"No, they don't."

"Yeah, you right. I picked that line from Jim." They laughed. Matt got serious and gazed into her eyes.

"Can I kiss you?"

"Yes, I would like that a lot?" Matt kissed Sheila, and she started to feel his dick through his pants. Matt stopped her.

"Remember, I told you, there is no rush. I'm okay with us just flirting and getting to know each other."

"I know...can I touch it?"

"You want to touch it?"

"I actually want to see it?"

"What?!"

"I never saw one before! I'm sorry."

Sheila started cracking up, and Matt stood there confused.

"You must think I'm weird as shit! It felt nice though."

"Oh, I get it now! You're trying to see if this White boy got a little dick?"

"No, no, no! That's not it."

"You don't even know how to lie right." He laughed.

"Come here. Touch it."

"No. Stop playing, Matt."

"I'm not playing. Touch it. I'm not scared of you."

Sheila got up to move the food and leaned him back on the bed. Sheila then proceeded to rub him between his legs.

"You like it?"

"Yes." She started kissing him and continued to rub.

"You don't seem new to this at all."

"No. I'm definitely new to this. I'm a virgin." Sheila held in a laugh.

"Oh, shit, really? Okay. I really need to ask you this, Sheila. Are you sure you want to do this?"

"This is my last time saying this, Matt. Yes."

"Okay."

Matt started to kiss her, and he completely turned her around facing him on the bed. He then lifted up her shirt, and Sheila helped assist. Sheila removed her bra, as Matt took off his shirt, his sneakers, and undid his pants. Sheila watched him carefully, ready to size him up to see if the myth was true. Sheila smiled because of the looks of things. She was lovin' what she saw.

"You look so good in your briefs."

"Oh, you like what you see, huh?"

Matt winked his eye at her, feeling very confident in size. Sheila sat back down on the bed, wearing only her panties. Matt knelt down in front of her and spread her legs. He then licked her in the middle, on top of her panties, and teased her on the outside. Sheila started to moan, as Matt pulled her panties to the side and went right in for the suck.

Sheila moaned, "Oh my God!" as Matt inserted his finger in her pussy and continued to suck. Sheila's legs trembled as he went in and out of her pussy vigorously with his finger, sucking and sucking until she announced she was about to cum. Just then, there was a panicked knock at the door. They both jumped and whispered to each other as their hearts raced.

Sheila yelled, "Who the fuck is it?!"

"Yo, I need to come in!"

They grabbed the covers to pull over them.

"This better not be a fuckin' joke!" Sheila got up and threw her clothes back on to open the door, opening it with attitude and walking away.

"Come the fuck in!" Jim came in, frantic.

"Matt, your roommate left several messages on my phone, man! Your dad was rushed to the hospital, and your mom needs you to come home right away!"

"What?!"

"Yeah, get dressed, and I'll wait outside for you. Here's the number to the hospital. Renee is calling to check on flights for you right now."

"Oh my God, Matt. Do you want me to go with you?"

"No. I'll be okay, hopefully. Can I call my mom? I'll pay for the call."

"Sure. You don't have to pay me back, Matt."

Matt hurried to place the call. He picked up the receiver and started dialing. He impatiently waited for an answer.

"Mom! What's up with Dad?!" He paused.

"I'm getting a flight right now. I'll be there tonight." He paused.

"Okay, love you, too!" Matt hurried to get dressed.

"I'm sorry, Sheila."

"What are you sorry for?! It's not your fault."

"I know. I don't know what else to say."

Sheila panicked as well.

"This is your dad you are talking about. Be safe, and call me if you need me to get there."

Matt stopped to kiss her and then finished getting dressed, putting on his pants and shirt. He opened the door for Jim, as he sat down to put on his sneakers. Sheila wrapped up in the blankets for comfort.

"If she can't find a flight for me tonight, I'm going to have to drive."

"No, I'll drive for you, man. I can't let you take that ride by yourself."

"Thanks, Jim. I really appreciate you."

"Bye, Gorgeous. I'll call you once I get some answers."

"Okay, I'll be praying for you and your family, Matt."

"Thank you, Gorgeous!" He kissed her and left.

Some time passes, and Renee walks into Sheila lying across the bed.

"What's up, friend? You worried about Matt?"

"Yeah, I hope it's not too serious, and his dad can make a full recovery."

"Damn, girl...it's always something. I'm beginning to think your ass is bad luck."

Sheila gave a serious tight-lipped stare at Renee. Renee quickly put her hands up.

"Sike, sike. I'm just playing with you, girl, damn. Just tryna make you laugh or at least put a smile on your face. You really look worried."

"Cause I am."

"Well, let's talk. It will take your mind off things. You must really like his ass, huh?"

"Yes, you can say that."

"Why are you so reserved with him?"

"Reserved?"

"Yes. It's like you half ass answer my questions when I talk about you

67

liking him. When it comes to Eric and Thaddeus, you never hesitated—not once—to say you liked them, but with Matt, it's all in your eyes—like you're scared to say it."

"No, I said I liked him."

"Yeah...but you always follow it up with a 'but he's white' afterwards."

"Really? It's that obvious?"

"Hell yeah, it's that obvious. That's why I'm telling you before he picks up on it."

"Well, honey...he knows how much I like him after today."

"Oh, shit, give me all the juice."

"Well...I think I was definitely about to cum. When Jim started to bang on the door, I felt something...it was this amazing feeling, I've never felt before. It was like a mixture of butterflies and the feeling I get when my pussy starts to tingle. It was taking everything out of me all at the same time. I've never felt like that before."

"Oh, damn. I've never felt like that before either. So, y'all asses was naked?"

"Yes, girl." She smiled.

"So, what it look like? Did it look like a little pink doggie dick or a little white thumb? What?" Renee asked excitedly

"No, Renee. It looked nothing like that. It was actually pretty."

"Pretty?"

"Yes. It reminded me of Thaddeus' dick but not as big—but not little either. It had a light skin kind of a complexion and soft pretty brown hair. I couldn't really see his balls, but I think they were darker than his dick."

"When you say, 'not a big as Thaddeus,' is it half Thaddeus' size? A tad bit smaller? Or a little more than half Thaddeus' size? Because, girl...you know everybody is talking about Thaddeus' horse dick. I don't know how you did it for the first time with a horse dick, but I've gotta give it to you!"
She high fived Sheila.

"I guess I don't know the difference between big or small. I don't know." Sheila was confused.

"So, can he fuck?"

"We didn't get that far."

"I thought you said you were about to cum…"

"Yeah, I was because he was eating the hell out of my pussy!"

"Yes! I told you! That's that freak shit I'm talking about!"

"Girl, I thought Thaddeus was good. Sheesh!"

"Oh, damn girl. So, White boys do eat some good pussy?"

"I don't know if it's a White boy thing, but I know Matt can."

"Look at you defending him and shit. I bet you are feeling that shit, as if he's still doing it, aren't you?"

"Whoo, yes!" She rubbed her hands between her legs.

"Want me to help you out with that?"

"Bitch, no!"

"Okay…I'm just tryna help a friend out."

"Yeah, okay! One day, I'm gonna catch your ass off guard, and sit right on your damn face."

Renee wiggled her tongue at Shelia.

"You know you like this tongue. Remember, this tongue was your first. Shit, we're in college, girl, and we're best friends. We're supposed to experience all this shit together!"

"No, actually, Thaddeus licked this pussy first!". Sheila corrected Renee.

"I know what I'm going to do…call Eric and tell him I can't sleep after all."

"Fuck it, I'll just stay here and watch then." Sheila ignored her.

"I'll just do what I always do, play sleep." Sheila still ignored her.

"I hope he got a little dick!" Renee yelled to be smart and laughed.

It's been months since she allowed anyone to get close to her. She was optimistic that Thaddeus would come back and pick up where they left off. With the help of Renee playing devil's advocate, Sheila snapped out of that fairytale and convinced herself to move on and seduce Matt. Sheila took heed to what Renee was saying and finally stepped out of her comfort zone. To her surprise, Matt gave Sheila amazing feelings that heightened her level of pleasure to another level she'd never felt before. Unfortunately, due to Matt's unfortunate situation, he had to leave—but with Sheila at a pleasurable peak, that wasn't going anywhere. She wanted and needed that feeling of satisfaction so badly that night; she called Eric and invited him back over. That night was the start of the two of them becoming inseparable for almost one year now.

Guess Who?

There was a knock at the door.

"Who is it?"

"Eric." Sheila opened the door.

"Hey, Baby, I missed you!"

Sheila's smile quickly left her face, as she noticed Thaddeus standing outside of Kay Kay's door. Thaddeus and Shelia gave each other eye contact, but Sheila quickly redirected it back on Eric. Eric backed Sheila into her room, kissing her all over her face, purposely blocking any view she had of Thaddeus and closed the door behind him.

"Damn, I don't get a hug?"

"Oh, sorry, Babe. My mind was somewhere else."

"Yeah, I know. Your mind was with that Thaddeus nigga."

"No, it wasn't. I am over his ass. It's been almost two years since we last talked. I was just caught off guard. He was the last person I expected to see when I opened my door, that's all."

Eric walked up to Sheila, looked her into her eyes, and kissed her softly on her lips.

"You better be over him. You're with me now, and I couldn't wait for us to get back to school, so I could see my girl."

"Yes, and I couldn't wait either to see my sexy chocolate bar."

"Well, you know chocolate melts in your mouth and not in your hands."

"Boy, you better get out of my face. I told you, I'm never going to suck dick!"

"Sike Sheila...you know I'm just playing."

"Yeah, you better be."

"You know I've been thinking all kinds of freaky shit being without you. Look what I got?"

Eric pulled out a VHS tape he had hidden under his arm in his jacket.

"Ooh, what movie is that?"

"A porno. This shit helped me get through my break over the summer."

"A porno?"

"Yes. Have you ever seen one before?"

"No."

"Here, put it in." He handed the tape over to Sheila.

"Oh wait, where's Renee?"

"She went to see Jim. It's not like she would be offended anyway." Sheila took the tape and put in the VCR and heard moaning the minute she pushed play on the tape. She saw a man fucking a woman bent over doggie style.

"Oh, shit! They're fucking!"

"Yeah, I left it right here at this part, so you can see nothing but action. This is how you learn all the new and latest tricks. It teaches you how to cum, eat pussy, and suck dick."

"Well, I told you I'm not sucking no dick, and I'm damn sure not eating any pussy!"

"I know. I'm not asking you to, Sheila. I was just telling you this is where you learn all that shit from."

"Mmmm...she is fuckin him good, like it's nothing."

"Does it turn you on?"

"I don't know. Let's keep watching. I think I'm more amazed than anything." Eric started kissing on Sheila's neck.

"Well, it's got me horny."

"Oh, really?"

"Baby, I want us to learn all this shit together."

"Well, there are some things I don't think I'll ever do, Eric."

"Yeah, that's what your momma said."

"What?" Eric laughed.

"I'm just joking, Baby. Whatever you want, Sheila, it's fine with me. If you don't want to do it, you don't have to. I have nothing but respect for you."

"I do have a question though, Eric?"

"What's your question?"

"If I don't give you oral, is there a possibility you will go and get it somewhere else?"

"That would be cheating, so no. I would never cheat on you. Like I said, I'm waiting for you until you are ready. I want us to be each other's first when it comes to doing that."

"You promise?"

"I promise. I wish I was your very first, but you were in love with Thaddeus at the time, so I understand why you gave that to him, but you never performed oral on anyone, and I want you to save that for me—your future husband."

"Husband? I like that. I've always wanted my husband to be my college sweetheart."

"Is that right?" asked Eric. The phone rang. Sheila answered it.

"Hello?"

"Hey, Gorgeous. How are you?" Sheila paused without saying anything.

"Sheila, I'm sorry. I know I haven't talked to you since the passing of my dad, but I was confused and totally shut down. Can you please allow me to come see you, so I can explain?"

Eric stood up and made his way over to Sheila. Sheila hurried and hung up the phone before he got close. Sheila quickly switched her phone to silent and walked away from it before Eric got there.

"Who was that?"

"Oh, nobody—them damn telemarketers."

"I'm hungry. You?"

"No, I'm horny."

"Oh. Well, I think that needs to be fixed."

Sheila walked up to him and started kissing him. Eric was super excited, and he started kissing her back and breathing heavy. Sheila felt him protruding through his pants and gave it a continuous rub.

"Damn. You really miss me?" Sheila whispered in Eric's ear.

"I haven't had none since break."

"You better not had."

Eric moved really fast taking off her shirt to suck her neck and breasts. Sheila moaned as Eric pulled her pants down, and quickly pulled her panties to the side to finger fuck her. Eric got up and took off his clothes. He pulled a condom out of his pocket, and Sheila laid back on the bed with her legs open. Eric quickly got on top of her, kissing her while at the same time penetrating her. He pulled up inside of her with a strong back, moaning as the feeling kept getting better. He pulled up, and pulled up, faster and faster, harder and harder.

"Oh, damn, Eric! You feel so good." Eric lost self-control and prematurely ejaculated.

"Oh, damn...I'm sorry baby." He apologized, trying to catch his breath.

"Sorry for what?"

"For cumming too fast," he explained breathing heavily.

"This is what happens when you don't have none in a while. That shit had me so excited, I couldn't hold it. Then, you started talking all sexy and shit...I knew it was a wrap!"

"As long as that's the issue, Baby, I'm okay with it. You better not be with nobody else."

"Oh, am I sensing a little jealousy?" He blushed.

"You better sense an ass whoopin' too if you do."

"I love my feisty, sexy Sheila."

"C'mon, let's get dressed and get something to eat."

"Yes, I'm starving now. Where do you want to go? The cafeteria? Or do you want to head over to Hardee's?"

"Let's head over to Hardee's."

Sheila went down the hall to wash up and brought a washcloth back to Eric, so he could get cleaned up as well. They got dressed, grabbed their jackets, and proceeded out the door. Renee was on her way in, as they made their exit.

"Hey, Sheila. Hey, Eric."

"Hey," they responded in unison.

"How are you doing, Renee?" Renee grabbed Sheila and pulled her back into the door.

"You can have her right back, Eric. Let me steal her for a second."

"Alright. As he stood outside the door."

"You know Matt is coming up for the weekend, right?"

"I'm not surprised. He just called, asking to see me in person, so he can explain why he hasn't called my ass in about a year."

"And...?"

"I hung up on his ass!"

"What? You fuckin' hung up on him!" Renee laughed.

"Yes, and I also put the phone on silent, so if you're expecting a call, switch it over." They both giggled.

"I still can't believe you hung up on him, girl."

"Girl, I didn't have a choice. Eric was coming over to see who I was talking to."

"Oh, shit! I've taught you well, quick thinking!" They giggled again.

"Okay, well, let me go. I'll see you when I get back. If Matt calls back again, tell him I'm upset and hurt and that it's hard for me to talk right now. Hopefully, that will buy me some time until I think of something."

Renee walks in wearing her cheerleading uniform, while Sheila does homework.

"Hey, what's up? Game over already?"

"No, I didn't feel well, Coach allowed me leave."

"Awww, what's wrong?"

"I think I'm coming down with something. I have a crazy headache and feel so drained."

"I have some Tylenol. You want one?"

"Yes, please."

Sheila got up to give her a Tylenol and some water.

"Here child, take this. Lie down, and rest."

"Girl, your bul was killing it on the courts today. It wasn't even halftime yet, and he had at least twenty something—almost thirty—points."

"That's nice."

"Stop acting like you don't care."

"I don't."

"So, why haven't you been to a game since you two broke up? I'm your girl, and he was your first—you care."

"I'm over him, Renee. What's up with all this talk about Thaddeus in the first place? I thought you had a headache?"

"I do have a headache, but he asked about you today, and I really need to know where you stand with him, before I tell you what I said?"

"Renee...what did you say?"

"Well, since you don't give a fuck...I told him you are fine and well, and you are madly in love with Eric."

"Oh, shit! No, you didn't."

"Yes, the fuck I did! I couldn't wait to bust his bubble."
Sheila laughed. He's been strolling around campus thinking he's the shit because all the bitches are on him. Well, not my girl! They laughed. You should've seen the look on his face after I slam dunked all that shit in it. They slapped high five and continued to laugh.

"Sheila, watch! That shit is gonna make him want you even more."

"Why you say that?"

"Men always want what they can't have."

"So, why did he leave me for an easy chick?"

"Well, technically, it wasn't like your ass was hard to get." Sheila got angry.

"Fuck you, Renee!"

"See...this is why my ass be lying to you because you can't handle the truth, Sheila. It's easier to just lie to your ass, brush it off, and go on about my day."
Sheila turned her back to Renee and continued with her homework.

"Oh, it's like that, Sheila?"

"Go ahead, and finish Renee."
Her arms were folded, and she had an attitude brewing.

"I'm not saying you were a fast ass or anything like that. He knew you were a virgin. He knew you were ready to lose your virginity, so he took advantage of that, and there was no chase."

"What do you mean, no chase?"

"My mom always told me, men love a challenge and how they will fight hard for what they can't have. I thought it was some bullshit to keep me from fuckin', but I found out the hard way, and that shit is true."

"I'm listening..."

"Look at my situation with Mike—even though I was a virgin, I just gave it up to him without a fight, and that nigga acted like he didn't know me after. Then, I teased Jim's ass with it and made him wait; now he wants to smell my ass every morning, afternoon, and night, and we're still going strong after two years."

"Well, I wish you would've been this honest with me before you cheered me into a fuckin' spree!"

"I did not cheer you on, Sheila. I was just showing you the ropes on how to go about things."

"Thanks for making me your little ho' project."

"I'm gonna chill on that note, before this conversation gets out of line. I'm sorry for being a friend."

Sheila turned around to do her homework, and Renee rolled over, pulling the covers over her head.

About an hour later, Sheila wakes Renee up by shaking her.

"Renee...? Renee...?"

"Yeah...?"

"I'm so sorry. I shouldn't have blamed you for what we talked about earlier. I didn't mean what I said. You just had me thinking, and it made me mad at myself for giving my virginity to the wrong person—a person who just said fuck me so quickly and went on to the next one. I shouldn't have taken it out on you like that. You taught me a lot friend, even some shit I don't think you should've showed me," Sheila laughed.

"But all that you taught me were all good experiences, and I'll never forget them." Sheila talked as she gently rubbed Renee's hair.

"Renee, do you hear me? Renee...? Damn, girl! I'm pouring my heart out to you, and your ass fell asleep on me."

Renee replied, in a sleepy voice, "I heard you, girl—you sorry, and you want me to suck your titty again." Sheila burst out laughing.

"What?! No, I didn't! Take your ass back to sleep. You are stupid." Sheila laughed.

In the morning, the alarm goes off, waking Eric and Sheila.

"Oh, shit! Get up Eric! We overslept and have to get to class!"

Eric jumped up out of his sleep.

"I don't know what happened? I had the alarm set, and it didn't go off for the time I set it for."

"We got 15 minutes. I'll see you at class. I'm just gonna leave on what I have on, brush my teeth and wash my face."

"Okay, I'll see you shortly."

They both went their different ways to get washed up and dressed. Sheila put on a robe and gathered her things to run down the hall to wash up. Eric grabbed his things to run over his dorm to wash up as well.

Then, 15 minutes later, Sheila made it to class on time but not Eric. As Professor Jones began, Eric came rushing in the door.

"I'm sorry, Professor Jones. I didn't mean to interrupt your class."

He sat next to Sheila, and they both giggled at each other.

"Whew! That was a close one."

"Messing around with you last night, we almost missed class," Sheila said with a flirtatious smile.

"Cut it out. I told you to stop, but you wanted to keep playing, so I had to give it to you." They both giggled as they flirted with one another.

"Excuse me, but do you two wish to share what's so funny with the rest of the class?" asked Professor Jones.

"Oh no, I'm sorry, Professor Jones. Please continue with the class. I'm sorry," Sheila apologized.

"Sheila, after class I need you to stay. I need to speak with you."

"Okay, Professor Jones."

Sheila wrote in her notebook, *Oh shit, what the fuck does he want?*

Eric leaned over, so he could see what she wrote down. Eric shrugged his shoulders. They both turned around to pay attention and continued on with class until it was over. After class, Sheila walked up to Professor Jones.

"Hi, Professor. You needed to speak with me?"

"Yes, have a seat. Last year, we struggled a little due to you sleeping in my class. Now this year, you started off great but now not so much. We are three months in, and you're starting to play a lot with Eric—as if you two are some high school teenagers. Why waste your parents' money, if you don't really want this? As of today, you're averaging a 71.0 in my class. If you do not pass this test on Monday and your final, you will fail. You need them both, so I suggest you stop playing and study. I need you to study hard and give your best this final month, so you can pass with at least an 80.0. That's about the best you can do in my class at this point. So, get your rest, study, and do what you have to do to pass my class.

"Do you understand?" Professor Jones asked firmly.

"Yes, Professor Jones, I do." Sheila left class upset.

"Is everything okay?" Eric asked.

"No, I'm in jeopardy of failing his class again, and if I don't give my all, I'm going to fail."

"No problem, Baby. I will help you study and do what we've gotta do to pass this class, okay? We've got a test next Monday. Let's start tonight and study throughout this weekend."

"Okay. Oh, shit! This weekend?"

"What's up with this weekend?"

"Oh nothing, I just promised a couple of girls I would braid their hair, that's all. That was just some extra money in my pocket, but I'm gonna have to cancel."

"Okay, well, that money can't compare to the price of what this class cost. C'mon, let's do what we gotta do and pass this class."

Eric walked Sheila over to the dorm, and as they came down the hall, Thaddeus is standing there talking to Kay Kay and Trina outside her door.

"Oh my God, why is he always here?"

"Why are you even worried about him? He doesn't even matter anymore. I'm here."

"I know. It's just getting on my nerves and starting to be all the time now. That's all."

As they passed them, the energy seemed a little intense. Thaddeus, Kay Kay and Trina stopped talking all of a sudden, as they watched Sheila and Eric walk by and go into the room. Sheila seemed to be annoyed, so Eric hugged her from behind and kissed her on her neck.

"Don't start. We are here to study—no more, no less." Sheila giggled, as she opened the door.

"Damn. I can't get a hug and a kiss from my girl?"

"Of course, you can, just making sure you don't have an ulterior motive behind all that hugging and kissing."

They both smiled at each other. Eric couldn't help himself; he kissed her again.

"Okay, that's enough!" She pushed him away. "C'mon, let's get to it and open these books, to do what we've gotta do."

Renee walked in and hurriedly grabbed her books.

"Hi, y'all! Bye, y'all! I have to go. I'm running late for class."

She left right back out in a hurry and closed the door behind her.

Sheila and Eric continued to study for the next two hours until they got tired.

"I'm gonna go over to my dorm and check on things. I haven't really been there since yesterday, other than the quick wash up this morning. After I see what's up over there, I'll come back and check on you later, okay?"

"Okay, I'm gonna take a quick nap anyway. I'm tired."

Eric gave her a kiss, grabbed his jacket, and left out the door. Sheila turned on the TV and lay down on the bed. Fifteen minutes later, she started to nod and fell into a deep sleep.

A few hours later, Sheila is awakened by a knock at the door. She quickly gets up!

"Who is it?"

"It's me, Baby." Sheila got up all discombobulated and answered the door.

"Awww, I'm sorry, Baby. You're still asleep."

"Hey, Eric. I'm so tired."

As she walked back to the bed, Eric stopped her and gave her a hug. Then, he directed her back to bed.

"Go ahead and go back to bed, Baby. All that studying got you tired as hell. Let me help you get comfortable and put your pajamas on you, Babe."

Eric took off Sheila's clothes and grabbed her pajamas to help her change out of her clothes.

"I'm gonna hang out with the fellas tonight. I'll check on you tomorrow."

"Okay," Sheila replied. "Be good!"

"Always." He smiled. Loving her jealousy, he tucked her in with a kiss and quietly left back out the door. Sheila fell back into a deep sleep.

A half hour later, there was another knock at the door.

"Who is it?" Sheila asked. There was no answer.

"Who is it?" There was no answer, again.

Sheila, now annoyed and tired, got up to answer the door. Sheila swung the door open with an attitude.

"I said, who the fuck is it?!"

"Hey, Baby, you miss me?"

Sheila took a deep swallow, trying not to look excited. She folded her arms and put on her angry face.

"What are you doing here, Thaddeus?" she asked very sternly.

"I miss you." He paused to stare into her eyes, looking for a reaction.

"I just wanted to see how you're doing?"

"You just saw me in the hallway earlier, so you know I'm doing just fine."

"You're not gonna ask me in?"

"No, what for?"

"Because you miss me, too."

"No, I don't."

"Yes, you do. I saw it all in your eyes when you walked pass me."

He pushed the door open and let himself in. Sheila's arms were still folded.

"I didn't invite you in, and I think it's best you leave."

"You know you don't mean that, Sheila."

"Stop playing with me! Yes, the fuck I do!"

Thaddeus walked up to Sheila and got in her face.

"Stop always tryna be so damn hard, Sheila. Look me in my eyes and tell me that. If you can, I'll leave."

Sheila looked up at Thaddeus and looked him in his eyes. As he looked back into hers, he waited for an answer. Sheila's eyes began to water. She turned her head to prevent him from seeing.

"Yeah, that's exactly what I thought," he said, closing the door.

"You want me, and I know you miss me, Sheila. Why you keep tryna fight it?"

"My boyfriend will be back soon."

"Yup, that's exactly what he is—a boy, and he better only be a friend. I'm your man, and I'm gonna always be your man. We'll have to let him know your true love is back, and his services are no longer needed."

"Um, excuse you? I'm not doing that to him."

"Did you fuck him?"

"That's none of your business."

"Yeah, you fucked him. I bet he can't make you feel like this."

"Thaddeus, no..."

She turned her head to resist his advances, but Thaddeus grabbed her chin and turned her head back around and kissed her. Sheila tried to resist again. Thaddeus gently started to kiss her down her neck and guided her hand down to the bulge in his pants.

"You feel that?"

"Yes," Sheila replied in a low voice.

"He missed you so much, Baby. And I know you missed him too, didn't you?"

Sheila refused to answer him. Thaddeus whispered close to her ear and asked her again.

"You missed him?"

"Yes." Thaddeus began to kiss her on the lips, really slow and gentle and wet.

"Nobody will ever know this body better than me." Renee walked in the door.

"Oh shit! What the fuck?! Thaddeus?"

"How you doing, Renee?"

"How the hell are you?! Does Gee Gee know you're in here?"

"Cut that shit out, Renee. She's not my girl, never have been and never will be."

"Well, you sure did act like she was, the day you left Sheila for her stank ass!"

"I didn't leave Sheila for her. I walked away from all that bullshit and drama. Sheila always wants to fight every got damn body and wouldn't calm the fuck down. I told her from the beginning, I don't like my girl out here fighting and acting like that. I was tired and mad, so I walked off, but not for no fucking Gee Gee! Gee Gee is everybody's girl; she bounces from dorm to dorm. Nobody wants to claim that. She's just cool to talk to, laugh and joke around with—that's it."

"Ummm hmmm, yeah...I guess that's your story, and you're sticking to it." Renee wasn't buying his story at all.

"That's what I was tryna tell your girl at the game that day." Sheila raised an eyebrow.

"Well, why did you lie and let her play me like that?"

"Play you how, Sheila?"

"You said you never fucked her."

"No, I didn't. You asked me did I used to talk to her, and I said no. Talking to her and fucking her are two different things."
Sheila thought back.

"Yeah, go ahead and think back, Sheila, with that feisty little brain of yours. I see it working. You never asked me that."
Sheila still tried to think back.

"Yeah, I fucked her, but that's all it was—a fuck."

"It must have been more than that because you left me for a whole year for her ass."

"What the fuck are you talking about? No, I didn't."

"Did you even try to come check on me?"
Sheila folded her arms and poked her lips out.

"Did you fuck her that night?"

"No, I ain't fuck her that night!"

"Why didn't you come to that party that night, huh? I didn't see you or Gee Gee."

"I didn't come because I was mad, hurt, and upset. I didn't feel like fuckin' partying! Oh, but what I did hear on the other hand? Somebody had one hell of a night, right? I don't know why you looking all confused, Sheila? You

84

remember everything else. Try to remember that!"

"I don't know what the fuck you're talkin' about, Thaddeus?"

"Well, let me refresh your memory, Sheila!" He got in her face.

"Anything white come to mind?" Sheila looked surprised.

"Yeah, it looks like you're remembering now. You were with your little White boyfriend, right Sheila? That's why I guess you never called to check up on me? Huh?"

Sheila turned her head and didn't answer. Thaddeus got up in her face to make her look at him.

"I heard he was all up on you!" Sheila didn't say a word.

"Yeah. I see it wasn't no problem for you to get over us that night." Sheila still remained silent with her arms folded.

"So, um, who loved who again?"

Putting his hand to his ear, he waited for Sheila to say something. But there was still complete silence.

"Yeah, that's what I thought! And that was the main reason why I didn't fuck with you no more. I was in my room hurting, and your ass was out partying all night, all in your little white boyfriend's face! I heard y'all was grinding all fucking night. Do you know how embarrassing that was to me, Sheila, to hear all that shit?"

Sheila was still silent with her head turned.

"My boys made me the joke of the night, telling me about 'my girl' and how she was having a fucking blast while I was sitting back hurting."

"Really, Thaddeus? I'm sorry." Sheila finally showed some kind of emotion. Feeling sorry for him, she gave him a hug.

"Hell yeah." Thaddeus turned around, and Sheila hugged him. Renee was quiet but was listening the whole time.

"Do you want me to leave you two alone? Jim has practice today, so I can always go back to his room. I'm sleepy anyway and need to get some sleep."

"You've been sleeping all day."

"I know. These classes got me so tired."

"I'm sorry, Renee, but can you? I'll call you and let you know when we're done."

"I guess you want me to get rid of Matt tonight when he gets here, right?" Renee whispered.

"Oh, shit! Yes. Tell him I went back home for the week for some family stuff. I know you'll hook it up."

"Okay, you know I gotcha."

Thaddeus walked around, observing the room, looking to see if he saw any changes since he was last there. Renee headed out the door.

"Okay, Sheila, I'll be back tomorrow."

"Okay, thank you, see you tomorrow!" Renee left out the door.

Thaddeus was still walking around, scoping the place and then picked up a VHS tape.

"Oh, you into watching porn now?"

"I don't watch it like that, just once in a while. This is actually my first porno tape ever."

"So, do you like it?"

"I guess so. You can learn a lot from it."

"Is that right? Okay, show me what you've learned."

"No. Technically, I'm still Eric's girlfriend, and I don't want to hurt him."

"Naw...fuck that shit. You're my girl. We never broke up, so "technically," since you want to be so damn technical, you're still mine."

"What? Are you kidding me? You haven't talked to my ass in over a year!"

"No, you stopped speaking to me."

"Why now, Thaddeus? Why are you so concerned about who stopped speaking to whom and who the hell I'm seeing?"

"What? This shit has been killing me for the longest. This didn't just start now. Since the day you left me, I started wondering."

"No, let me stop your ass right there. I didn't leave you. Your ass left me, remember?"

"Sheila, c'mon, let's stop it with this whole blame game. I miss you, and I love you."

Sheila started to tear up.

"I want my girl back. I've tried to get you out of my mind, but I can't. No one can ever replace my Sheila."

"Did you just say you love me?"

"Yeah, I did, and I'm not afraid to admit it anymore. I have to stop keeping all these feelings I have for you to myself."

"Thaddeus, you've gotta give me a chance to think this over."

"I need my baby, now." Thaddeus plead and tried to hug Sheila, but she resisted and pulled back to finish talking.

"Thaddeus, you can't just come in here and reverse a year just like that."

"Do you love me?" asked Thaddeus

"That's not the point."

"Do you love me?"

"Yes, I do. But it doesn't change the here and now, Thaddeus." Thaddeus ignored her, as he persisted on hugging her.

"Well, then show me, Sheila. Please, Baby."

"Thaddeus...you've still gotta give me some time to figure this all out. This is not Eric's fault, and he shouldn't get hurt throughout all of this."

"You have one day to figure out how you're gonna break the news to him."

"No, Thaddeus. C'mon, I can't do that. You waited over a year to come all up in here to confess your love and how you feel for me. You can give me a couple of months to break it off with Eric."

"A couple of months?!"

"Yes."

"Why so long? Hasn't it been long enough for us?"

"I don't want him to think it's because of you. Eric is a good dude, and it will allow me the time I need to ease away."

"Two months...but he can't have no more of my little pussy, alright?" Sheila doesn't say anything.

"Alright?"

"Alright, Thaddeus."

"You promise?"

"Yeah...yeah."

"Meanwhile, come over here, and show me how much you really miss me." Sheila walked over and started to kiss Thaddeus. She proceeded down to his neck and took off his shirt to kiss his chest and down to his navel.

"I thought you learned a lot from watching porn?" asked Thaddeus.

"I've learned a little something."

"Show me."

Sheila didn't want to disappoint, so she proceeded to give Thaddeus what he was asking for.

"I'm gonna show you how much I've missed you."

Sheila went down into a squatting position and pulled down his sweats. Thaddeus' dick was so erect with clear semen right at the tip.

"Take your clothes off." Thaddeus was overly excited and quickly took his clothes off.

"I'm ready, Baby."

"Wait, I'm sorry. I really want to, but I don't know if I can do this, yet."

"What's wrong? Don't you love me?"

"Yes, I love you."

"Then show me. I'll talk you through it."

"No. Don't let me do this."

Sheila went back down and wiped the tip of his dick with her finger. She hesitated for a minute but opened her mouth and placed his dick on the tip of her tongue. Thaddeus' eyes began to close, as he started to moan.

"Your tongue is so warm, Baby. You just don't know how excited this got me. Put it all the way in your mouth, and suck it baby."

Sheila got irritated, as she slowly put it in her mouth. She quickly pulled it back out and wiped the semen she tasted off her tongue. Thaddeus got excited and grabbed her head, pulling it forward. Sheila resisted and pulled away.

"Wait a got damn minute, and let me do it!" Sheila exclaimed.

"Are you sure this your first time?"

"Yes, this is my first time."

"Yeah, better be. I better be your first in everything. You hear me?"

"Mmmm hmmm."

Sheila is flattered by Thaddeus' jealousy. Now, she's more motivated than ever to please him. She put his dick back in her mouth to try again.

"Oh, Baby, you feel so good. Let me show you how to suck this dick."

"What the fuck? I said let me do it!"

"I'm sorry, Baby. I'm just so excited because I've missed you so much, and you're making me feel good. I'm your man. We should be able to share things like this together and learn from each other." Sheila attempted to suck.

"Oh, shit…make sure your teeth don't touch. Cover them with your lips, and bring your tongue up to suck it at the same time."
Sheila was irritated, but she complied this time.

"Oh yeah, Baby, just like that." Sheila proceeded and then got into a rhythm.

"Oh shit, Baby, you feel so good!"
Sheila began to hear him moan, like she never heard him moan before and felt a sense confidence about giving oral for the first time. Thaddeus began to pull her head in harder to fuck her mouth. As it started to get real good to Thaddeus, he began to pull her head in faster and faster. Sheila tried to pull away, but Thaddeus got excited and continued fucking her mouth harder and harder, deeper and deeper, with a tight grip.

"Oh, shit! I'm about to cum, Baby! I'm about to fuckin' cum!"
Sheila tried to pull away, but Thaddeus' grip was too tight. He pushed his dick deep down in her throat, and Sheila started to gag and until she threw up everywhere.

"Yuck!" Sheila coughed and gagged, while Thaddeus finished off the job ejaculating with his own assistance.

"Damnit, Thaddeus! I told you to stop!" she yelled, spitting continuously.

"I'm sorry, Baby. That shit felt so good. I didn't know how to control it." Sheila was still spitting.

"You got a towel or something to clean it up with?"

"Yes. Get the towel from behind the door and another one in my bottom drawer for you."
Thaddeus threw her a towel and got one for himself.

"Now take that bucket over there in the corner, go down to the bathroom, and put some water in it for me, please. I'll try to start cleaning it up in here, as much as I can."

"While I'm down there, I'm gonna wash up real quick to get the spit up off me."

"Thaddeus, make sure you lock the door behind you, please. You can get me in trouble if someone catches you in there, and to top it all off, you're naked, too."

Sheila started thinking. Wait a minute, maybe I should go.

"Sheila, it's late. Who's taking a shower this time of night? You got that shit all over you and still have to clean up the rest of it. After cleaning all that shit up, I know you're gonna want to shower. So, let me go ahead and get mine outta the way because I'll have to do it regardless. I can't go back to my room like this."

"Okay, okay. Just be careful, and hurry up. Take this towel, and rinse it out for me with some soap and water."

"Damn! This shit stinks!"

Thaddeus proceeded to walk down the hallway with a towel and a bucket. He slowly opened the bathroom door and looked around to make sure no one else was in there.

"Is anyone in here?"

No one answered. Thaddeus snuck in, took off his towel, and hurried to take a quick shower. Trina walked in wearing only a towel.

"Oh, you just couldn't wait to get your ass next door, could you?"

Thaddeus looked up at Trina, tryna cover up.

"Oh shit, I forgot to lock the door!"

Trina stood there, looking at Thaddeus and smiled.

"What does she have that I don't?"

Thaddeus stood there quietly, watching Trina's every move. Trina purposely dropped her towel and walked over to Thaddeus.

"You look confused or something. You need some help because your ass stinks?"

Trina turned on the water over Thaddeus' head in the shower. She then picked up the soap to lather her hands and proceeded to wash him up with her hands. Trina looked down and noticed Thaddeus was starting to get erect.

"Hmmm...Nice and big. I've never had a dick that big before."

Thaddeus started to get excited but remained silent.

"I think he's happy to see me, after all. I was worried that he didn't like me."

"You're not scared of someone coming in?"

"No, because unlike you, I'm smart enough to lock the door."

"Did you see me come in here?"

"I sure did. Is that a problem?"

Thaddeus didn't respond as Trina turns around.

"Will you wash my back for me, please?"

Trina backed up so close to him, she felt a brush of his dick touch her ass from behind. Thaddeus reluctantly complied and started to rub her back with the soap. Trina moaned and seductively began to talk.

"Oh, Thaddeus, that feels so good. Your hands are so strong but soft at the same time."

Trina took another slow step back and purposely rubbed her soapy ass on Thaddeus' dick. Thaddeus rubbed his dick between the crack of her ass, as Trina enjoyed the power she had being able to control his mind and body. Thaddeus started to grind and push into the crack of her ass even more. Thaddeus got excited and bent her soapy ass over, vigorously grinding at the entrance of her pussy.

"Yeah, Baby, fuck me! I've been waiting for this dick for so long."

Thaddeus finally got his dick all the way in and fucked her like a prison scene. Trina was trying not to scream as Thaddeus continued to fuck her good and hard.

"Oh, shit, this dick is so big!"

"You wanted this dick, right?"

"Yes!"

"Fuck me back!"

"Turn me around."

"No, you're gonna take all this dick!"

He continued fucking her faster and faster, harder and harder, until he exploded all in her pussy.

"Damn you, Thaddeus! What the hell was that?!"

Thaddeus pulled out and took a deep breath, putting his index finger to his lip, signaling her to bring her voice down a notch. Trina lowered her voice to an angry whisper.

"You act like you never had pussy before!"

Thaddeus laughed at what she said, still breathing hard, trying to get himself together.

"That shit ain't funny!"

"You said you wanted it." He continued to laugh.

Trina pushed him, picked up her towel, and headed out to leave. She continued to fuss at him, all the way to the door.

"Hey, don't you wanna wash that thing first before you leave?"

"No! Got my pussy all sore and shit!"

"C'mon Trina, keep it down. I gave you what you asked for, damn." Thaddeus laughed as Trina left out and slammed the door. Thaddeus started to wash himself, still laughing.

"Thaddeus!" Sheila's voice startled him.

"Oh shit, you scared the shit out of me!"

"What the hell is taking you so long? Did I just see Trina's ass leaving out of here?"

"Yeah, Babe, don't get mad. I forgot to lock the door, and I scared the shit out of her when she came in." He laughed.

"You should've seen her face."

"Did she see you naked?"

"Oh, no. I put the towel around me once I heard the door open."

"Awww, shit! I hope she doesn't get my ass into any trouble. I told you to lock the damn door. Damn!"

"I know. I'm sorry, Baby."

"Yeah, yeah. Move over, so I can wash this stinking ass shit off of me."

Decision, Decisions

Renee slowly roll over, squinting her eyes.

"Renee, get your ass up!"

"What time is it?"

"4:50!"

"Oh my God, Sheila. Why are you yelling?"

"I'm not yelling. I'm hype."

"Hype about what?"

"You! You are late damn near every day now for everything—classes, cheerleading practice—you name it!
What? You just don't care anymore? Are you giving up?"

"Hell no, I'm not giving up. I think I'm coming down with something. I got some kind of flu, virus—I don't know what the fuck it is, but I can't wait until this shit goes away."

Sheila felt Renee's head.

"Well, you do feel a little warm. Do you need me to get something for you?"

"No, Jim just went to the store to get me some soup, ginger ale, and crackers."

Renee put her hand over her nose.

"Bitch, where you coming from? You stink."

"Track."

"Go wash or something," she started to gag.

"Oh my God! Grab the bucket, I think I gotta throw up!"

Sheila grabbed the bucket really quickly, as Renee hurried to lean over it.

"Awww, Renee, you are really sick. Lay your ass back down and get your rest. I'll talk to your coach tomorrow and let her know. If you don't feel better by Monday, I'll talk to your professors as well. But I think you really need to get a checkup; this has been going on for some time now."

"Ok, thanks girl. Now can you please take shower?"

"Damn. I don't smell that bad."

"Hmmm..." Renee said, twisting her lip.

"Okay, I'm going."

"Sheila, I know this is nasty, but can you dump this bucket for me."

"Hell yeah, that shit is nasty, but I guess…anything for my best friend."

"Oh my God, I just love you!"

Sheila smiled, as Renee blew her a kiss, closed her eyes, and pulled the blanket back over her head. Sheila then gathered her things and left out to take a shower.

The phone rang. Renee tried to ignore it. The phone rang again. Renee fussed but got up to answer it.

"What?!"

"Hey, Baby, I'm on my way back."

"Okay, you know I'm sick. Did you have to call and tell me something I already know?"

"No, with your smart ass. I'm calling to see if it's cool to bring Matt. He just got up here and is dying to see Sheila."

"Oh okay. She's in the shower, but I don't see anything wrong with it. Bring him."

"You sure?"

"Yes," Renee said annoyed. "Now I'm going to lay back down until you get here."

"I'm sorry, Baby. Go back to sleep. See you in 15-20 minutes."

"Bye, Jim."

Renee hung up the phone and rolled back over under the blanket. The phone rang again. She jumped up very irritated.

"Jim, just come the fuck on and stop calling!"

"Hello? Everything okay? This is Eric." Renee paused for a second.

"Eric? Oh, shit. I'm sorry. I'm not feeling well, and the phone keeps ringing while I'm trying to get some sleep."

"Oh, I'm sorry."

"It's not your fault. You didn't know."

"Is Sheila there?"

"No. She's somewhere. I'll tell her to call you when she gets in."

"Okay, yeah, I'm tryna catch her before she starts doing hair."

"Come to think of it, she did mention that. Sorry, I was half asleep."

Sheila walked in the room as Renee put her finger to her lip, signaling her to hush.

"She did say she was going to do somebody's hair, damn."

"It's okay, Renee. I'll talk to her later. Get your rest."

"Okay Eric, goodbye." Sheila's eyes lit up.

"Oh, shit! That was Eric?"

"Yeah." Renee put the covers back over her head.

"So, why did you hang up on him? What he say?"

"He wanted to talk you before you did hair. So, I told him you started already to give you plenty of time to talk to Matt."

"Matt?!"

"Look, damnit! I am tired, and I'm delirious right now. Yes, Matt. He's on his way over here with Jim, and they should be walking in any minute."

"What am I going to tell Thaddeus if he finds out?"

"Fuck Thaddeus! He should be the least of your worries. You should be more worried about Eric than anything."

"Well, what am I going to tell Matt? I didn't get a chance to think of anything, and he's gonna wanna know why I've been ignoring his calls?"

"Hmmmm...am I detecting you've found a spot in your heart for Matt?"

"For some reason, I do miss him, and I didn't even give him none yet."

"Maybe it's the curiosity that's got you excited? I don't know, but for the last time, I'm gonna get back to my rest."

"No, Renee. I need you for a sec. Help me think of something."

"Just play hurt. Let him hug you and shit. He'll blame himself, and it will all work out."

"Renee. His dad died, have some kind of sympathy for him. It would be real selfish of me to use reverse psychology at a time like this."

"Well, give him some pussy, and I bet he'll forget all that shit."

"Renee, that's some real fucked up shit to say."

"Oh, hush girl, I bet it will work."

Renee rolled back over as Sheila got dress.

There was a knock at the door. Sheila got up to answer it.

"Who is it?"

"It's me, Jim."

Sheila opened the door and stood there, until they are all the way in. Jim came in, Matt behind him.

"Hey, Sheila."

"Hey, Matt."

Sheila turned her head to show no interest.

"I'm sorry, Sheila. I shouldn't have shut you out like that. When my dad died, it wore me down mentally and took me to a place I've never been before."

"But why would you totally shut me out like that? Did you think I would've made matters worse?"

"No, not at all. I wasn't thinking. I wasn't in my right state of mind. My dad meant everything to me, and that's what it felt like I lost...everything. It got to the point, Sheila, that I wanted to be with him. I was actually wishing death on myself. I was feeling like what's the use of living?" Matt put his head down in disappointment, thinking back on this sad moment in his life.

"So, you were contemplating on suicide?" asked Sheila.

"As embarrassing it may sound, yes."

"How do you feel now?" Sheila held his hand as Renee interrupted.

"Crazy as hell! Look, I think I've made a mistake. You know what, right now may not be a good time for y'all to start seeing each other." Sheila got mad instantly.

"Renee, stop it."

"What the fuck are you doing?" asked Jim.

"I'm saving my girl."

"Saving her from what, Renee? asked Matt.

"And for your damn information, I'm not crazy. I just went through something that was real traumatic for me. Have you ever lost someone before, your mother or father?"

The room got quiet. Renee shook her head no.

"Well, until you lose someone you thought you could never live without, don't judge me. Jim, I'm sorry for cursing at your girl like that, but..."

Jim cutting him off, "No need to apologize man. She had that coming. I'm sorry. I'm gonna take her little ass for a walk, while you and Sheila catch up.

Meet me back at my dorm when you are done."

Jim grabbed Renee by her arm and directed her to the door.

"Jim!" yelled Renee.

"Jim, my ass. Bring your ass on, Renee!"

"This is why my psychiatrist wanted me to distance myself from people for a while. He wanted to make sure I was ready to handle discussions like this."

"Psychiatrist?"

"Yeah, my mom wanted me to see someone. I was going through depression, and he actually saved my life. That's what I've been doing for the past 13 months. I stopped going to school and totally cut myself off from society during my time of grieving."

"Awww Matt, I'm so sorry to hear that. I feel bad for being so angry with you."

"I don't blame you. My mom wouldn't let you talk to me, and she wouldn't give you an explanation, so I totally get why you were angry. It's been months since we last spoke."

"It sure has. Give me a hug," asked Sheila, and they hugged real tight.

"Oh, Sheila, I miss your hugs."

"I miss your hugs, too, Matt."

"I bet someone scooped you up, didn't they?"

"No, I've just been dating here and there, nothing serious. Wait a minute, hold up! Did you just say scooped me?"

"Yeah, I did." Picking up on his slang, Sheila and Matt laughed.

"So, how long are you here for?"

"I just came up to see you for the day. I'm going back tonight."

"That's all you came here for?"

"Yes, ma'am."

"What if I had a boyfriend or something, laying up in here when you came?"

"Well, that was a chance I was willing to take. I needed to explain my situation to you in person, and I needed to see your beautiful face again." Sheila blushed.

"Sheila, will you give me another chance? I want to start all over with you from the beginning and see where we can take this."

"Sure, Matt. I would like that."

"Awesome!" Sheila laughed, as Matt gave her a big hug.

"Well, I got what I came here for. I have exactly what I need to hold me over, until the next time I see your pretty smile again. I'm gonna get the next flight back and get home before my mom worries."

"When are you going back to school?"

"Next semester. Then, I'll be only an hour away. And, trust me, Babe, you are gonna get sick of me then."

"Okay, we'll see."

"Can I kiss you?"

"Absolutely."

"Oh, absolutely? Sounds like something I would say, but I'm not judging." They both laughed and kissed, as she walked him to the door.

Sheila and Eric are chilling, watching TV in her dorm when there's a hard knock at the door, making them both jump.

"You want me to get that for you, Babe?" The knock got harder.

"Yo! Who the fuck is that? Let me get that!" Eric exclaimed.

"No. I'll get it."

Sheila cracked the door open and as she tries to step out, Thaddeus pushed the door open and stormed into the room.

"Thaddeus, what are you doing?!" Sheila yelled

Thaddeus walked right past her and headed straight toward Eric.

"Yo, dude! It's time for you to roll."

"Yo, who the fuck you think you talkin' to?" Eric replied.

"I'm talkin' to you!" Sheila jumped between them and pushed Thaddeus back.

"I got this, Babe." Eric put his arm out to block Sheila from being in the middle.

.   "Thaddeus, I told you to let me handle this!" Sheila exclaimed.

"Whoa! Hold up, wait a minute!" Eric turned to Sheila. "What you mean, let you handle this?"

"Give me a minute, Eric." Sheila replied.

"No, I want to know now. What do you mean by 'handle this,' Sheila?"

"See, that's exactly why I came in here, Sheila! You mean to tell me, after three months, you ain't said shit?"

"No, I haven't. It's not that simple, Thaddeus."

"What the fuck you mean, it's not that simple?" yelled Eric.

"Well, let me simplify this shit for you! Got me all hype, about to fight this dude—trying to have your fuckin' back, thinking he's disrespecting you, and here, I'm the one being disrespected?!"

Sheila got quiet and didn't say a word.

"Hmmm...let me guess? You seeing him again?"

Sheila put her head down.

"Wow, this is all starting to make sense now. All this talk about saving yourself and not having sex with me anymore was all bullshit. Damn. You played the shit out of me. What the fuck did I do to you to deserve this shit, Sheila? I'm up here lovin' you like crazy, proud to have you as my girl, thinkin' I've hit the jackpot. I've never disrespected you, always respected all your wishes, never cheated on you, and you do me like this?"

Sheila remained quiet with her head down, as Eric let out a sarcastic laugh.

"It's always the good guys. I'm not gonna front, this shit hurts like hell."

Eric started to gather his things.

"Let me get the fuck out of here, before I get my ass kicked out of school over some bullshit, especially when the feelings aren't mutual."

Eric looked at Sheila as he walked to the door and past everyone who was standing in the hallway, watching and being nosey.

"Thaddeus!" Sheila punched him, as he tried to hold her hands.

"Let me close the door, Sheila, so we can talk about this."

She continued to throw punches. He grabbed her into a bear hug.

"Close the door, somebody!" He yelled, and the door is push closed.

"Sheila, I love you, and I couldn't see you with that guy anymore." Sheila started crying.

"I didn't want to hurt him like that. He was always good to me."

"You rather for me to hurt?"

"No, I'm not saying that. There was just a better way to handle this, Thaddeus. That's all."

"I'm sorry, Baby. You don't have to worry about hurting anyone's feelings from this point further because it's you and me from this point on."

"You don't understand, Thaddeus."

"You just don't play with people feelings like that."

"I'm sorry. Come here, Baby."

He pulled her over to the bed, held her, and let her cry.

Later, Renee walks into the dark room where Sheila and Thaddeus are asleep, holding each other in the bed. Renee turns on the light.

"What the fuck am I hearing went on in this room earlier?!"

"Hey, Renee. I'll talk to you about it later."

Renee ignored Sheila's request.

"Why the fuck you do that shit to Eric, Thaddeus?"

"I got tired of seeing him with my woman."

"Oh, just like she got tired of seeing you around campus with all of your women, huh?"

"I got this Renee."

"Yeah, okay, Sheila. I just don't think it's fair for him to tell you how to act, but when you see bitches all up in his face. But it's okay for him to act a fool when he sees you with someone. You don't even owe him a damn thing, no explanation or nothing because he's not even your man!"

"Renee," Sheila cut her off.

"I know, and I understand your frustration. We've talked all about that."

"Well, I hope you made the right decision, friend because Eric was good to you. This mutha'fucka right here ain't nothing but a damn dog."

"Damn, Renee. It's like that? I thought we were cool?" Thaddeus asked.

"Not cool enough to compromise my best friend's happiness. No, we ain't the fuck cool! From this point forward, I'm gonna be all over your ass, so you better not make one fuckin' mistake. If you do, I better not hear shit come out of your mouth about acting like a fuckin' lady either, when I come for your ass, and you best believe a lady, I will be not!"

"Renee, you've got my word. I love your girl. I would never purposely hurt her."

"On purpose, accidentally, I don't give a fuck!" Sheila cut her off.

"Renee!" Renee with her hands on her hips, answered with an attitude. "What Sheila?"

"I thought you were staying over Jim's."

"I was...but that nigga stinks!" Renee said, with an attitude.

"What?" Sheila and Thaddeus laughed.

"Yeah, I don't know what the fuck it is, but he stinks all of a sudden to me, him and his damn room!"

"So, now what?"

"It made me sick, so I left. But as I was coming back to our room, I got an ear full about Thaddeus and his bullshit."

Thaddeus shook his head and threw up his arms.

"I'm gonna give you two some time to talk. I'm gonna get something to eat. I'll be back a little later."

"Okay." Thaddeus kissed her before he exited.

"See that bullshit right there?"

"What? Him wanting to leave to get something to eat?" asked Sheila.

"No, the fact that he didn't ask you if you wanted anything. Selfish ass nigga. I'm going to bed."

Renee is in the room chilling. Sheila comes in with her head down.

"Hey, what's with you, Sheila?"

"I just found out I failed my test today, which means I pretty much failed my Psychology class. My mom and dad are going to kick my ass!"

"No, they're not. I got you. We're gonna fix this."

"How?"

"You can take a night class next semester."

"How am I gonna keep them from getting my grades? And where am I gonna get the money for a night class?"

"Well, I can pull something out of my sleeve to stop the grades from getting to them—girl, so that's the least of our worries."

"How are you going to do that, Renee?"

"Girl, I can get Mr. Kennedy in admissions to fix that shit, and if he can't, I'll get my mailman friend to just throw that shit away."

"What? Come again?"

"Well, I always catch Mr. Kennedy looking at my ass when I'm in his office. I can get his little perverted ass to do just about to do anything, but if that doesn't work, I'll go with plan B and get our mailman to throw that shit away." Sheila raised an eyebrow.

"Oh, his ass likes me, too." They both laughed.

"Renee, you are a damn mess. I don't know what I'm gonna do with your ass, girl. I don't know if I should love you or hate your ass." Sheila laughed.

"Oh, you will never hate me, girl."

"Yeah, girl, I know."

"I can't believe I failed though. I barely passed his class last year, and now this year, I'm fuckin up again. I guess Professor Jones is giving me a damn lesson this time. He really worked with me the last year, giving me extra credit to get through. And what did I do? Take advantage of his kindness and play around again."

"See if he'll give you extra credit again before finals."

"I already asked, and he quickly said no. That's why I know he's giving me a lesson, and boy I am quickly learning. He wants me to get my shit together for next year, and I understand. It's no one's fault but mine. Damn. I wish Eric was here to help me through this. He is smart as shit, always acing his tests, and I don't even know when he found the time to study!"

"Yeah, I hate that shit. People like him are like a damn sponge. They remember everything they learn, but my ass gotta go over shit a million times in order to get it."

"Well, Honey, I need you to work your magic and stop those grades, and I guess I'll have to get my ass working on getting this money up."

"I have a little extra money to contribute."

"Awww, thanks friend."

"I'll get some from Jim as well."

"Oh, that will be awesome!"

"Awesome, Bitch?!" Renee laughed.

"Did I say awesome?"

"Yes, you did." Sheila laughed.

"Oh, shit—that's Matt wearing off on me."

They both laughed.

"Thanks for cheering me up, girl. I was lost there for a minute. By the way, I'll get Matt and Thaddeus to donate as well."

"Thaddeus' ass needs to come up with all of it. It's his fault Eric wasn't here to help you. He wanna be all up in the pussy, make him be all up in the bills, too."

"Yes, I'll ask his ass first."

Sheila picked up the phone to call Thaddeus, and a girl's voice answered.

"Hello?" The phone quickly hung up.

"Hello? Hello?" Sheila redialed and impatiently waited for an answer. She redialed again and again but no answer.

"Oh., fuck this! I'm taking my ass over there."

"What? What's wrong?"

"A bitch answered his phone, and then just hung up!"

"Oh, fuck that! C'mon!"

Sheila and Renee headed out the door and over to Thaddeus' room. They saw Thaddeus midway over, and he noticed Sheila was clearly upset.

"Who the fuck you have in your room, Thaddeus?"

"Huh? What are you talking about, Sheila?"

"I just called your room, a bitch answered, and then hung up on me."

"I wasn't in my room, Sheila. Dwight is in there with his girl. Maybe it was her? I don't know. I was on my way to see you."

"Bullshit!" Renee intervened.

"Fucking liar! I know a lying ass when I see one!"

"You should, Renee, cause you're the best at it!" Sheila replied.

"This shit ain't about me, Sheila! It's about this lying ass nigga. I'm here tryna defend you, and you turn this shit on me."

Thaddeus intervened, "What fuck are you two talking about?"

Sheila replies to Renee, "I'm just calling it as I see it, Renee. I'm not turning on you."

"You know what, Sheila? I'm about sick of you being all turned the fuck out over this nigga! I'm starting to believe you actually enjoy smelling his shit! You gonna let this mutha'fucka come between us, Sheila—turning this shit on me? Well, I'm not gonna allow it!"

"Renee, calm the fuck down. It's not that damn serious! Why are you getting all hype and shit? I only spoke the truth. You know you're a damn liar."

"Well, if you feel so strongly about speaking the truth, you need to start with this nigga right here!"

She pointed to Thaddeus, and he intervened.

"I didn't do anything, Renee."

Thaddeus replied, throwing his hands up.

"What did I do to make you hate me so much?"

"Fuck you, Thaddeus! I'm gonna get your ass, nigga! My girl may be sprung on your ass, but not me! I hope you're making the right decision, Sheila."

Sheila doesn't say anything. Renee stormed off and headed toward the boys' dorm.

Sheila yelled, "Where the fuck is you going, Renee?"

"Over Jim's. Now, leave me the fuck alone!"

"Renee, c'mon!"

Renee was not tryna hear it and continued to storm off.

Two months later, Renee comes storming inside the room.

"Sheila, bitch! Where the fuck is Thaddeus?"

"I don't know, why?"

"Girl, I knew that fuckin' nigga wasn't shit!"

"Renee, what?"

"Wait. This got me so upset. I feel like I'm gonna throw up."

Sheila grabbed a bucket and handed it to her.

"Is it that bad?"

Renee put up her finger to suggest Sheila wait a minute. There's a knock at the door. Sheila opened the door, as Jim rushes in.

"Sheila, you alright?"

"Yes, why?"

"What's wrong with Renee?"

"She said she feels like she gotta throw up."

"Damn, that shit got you like that, Renee? C'mon, Baby, lay down."

There's another knock at the door. Sheila went to answer it. Thaddeus came rushing in.

"Oh, I see you beat me to it," asked Thaddeus.

"Jim, get his ass!" yelled Renee.

Renee gagged and quickly shut back up.

"What you mean, beat you to it? This is my girl, my best friend—she's like a sister to me."

"She can tell her whatever the fuck she wanna tell her," Jim interjected.

"I'm not saying that," Thaddeus replied.

"Well, what are you saying?" asked Jim.

"I just want the opportunity to talk to her myself, that's all."

"Well, they're best friends, and when it comes to them two protecting one another, they're not gonna wait. They're gonna handle it right then and there. If you don't know how these two roll by now, you don't know your girl."

"Will somebody please tell me what the hell is going on?!" asked Sheila.

Jim continued talking, tuning her out.

"I know if I ever did anything, I'm already prepared to get it from both their asses. That's why I don't do shit."

"Oh, I guess you're gonna sit and act like your shit don't stink?"

"No, my shit stinks. I just don't shit on my girl."

Sheila stood there with her arms folded, listening to them go back and forth.

"Hello? Ummm...do you have something to tell me?"

Thaddeus grabbed Sheila by the hand and pulled her to the side.

"Sheila baby, damn...it's some bullshit going on."

"I'm listening."

"People out here just hate seeing us happy."

Renee jumped up to intervene.

"Sheila, this nigga got two bitches pregnant!"

"Just one," Thaddeus replied, "...and I'm not sure if it's mine."

"Two!" Renee repeated.

Sheila put her hand to her forehead in disbelief. She got stuck in a stare as she started to tear up.

"Mind your fucking business, Renee!" yelled Thaddeus.

"Nigga, I'll break your fucking jaw." Jim jumped in Thaddeus' face.

"Oh, okay. Y'all just gonna gang up on me like that?"

"You're not gonna to talk to mine like that, that's all I know."

"Sheila, talk to me."

Sheila pulled away, as he tried to pull her closer to him. Jim intervened.

"She doesn't want to be bothered."

"You deal with yours, and let me deal with mine."

Jim tried really hard not to punch Thaddeus in his face.

Renee got up to hold Sheila's hand.

"Sheila, this nigga got two kids on the way—one by Gee Gee and the other by Trina."

"I only have one baby that's in question, Sheila...and I'm just finding out about this shit myself. I never cheated on you. This situation happened while we weren't together."

Sheila remained quiet, just crying and listening. Renee tried to talk and stay calm to keep from getting upset.

"Sheila, the reason he came back to you was because Gee Gee is home. She went home for break and stayed because she's pregnant, and from what I hear, she's damn near due."

Sheila wiped her eyes with her hands.

"Is this true, Thaddeus?"

"Not everything."

"Well what part isn't true?"

"Ummm, I didn't come here to be with you because she left."

"So, it's your baby?"

"I don't know. Gee Gee was fuckin' everybody."

"Including you...and without a fuckin' condom!"

"It was only once Sheila, to get back at you for seeing Eric. You think I didn't hear about you two!?"

"I don't give a fuck what you heard about me. We weren't together, and I could pretty much do whatever the fuck I wanted to do!"

"And so could I!"

"Well, why the fuck you lie to me then?! I've asked you over and over again about Gee Gee, and all you did was deny being with her."

Renee intervened.

"Don't forget about Trina's ass, Sheila!"

"Trina?! Where the fuck does Trina come into this at? Huh?" Sheila gets in Thaddeus' face.

"I don't know, Sheila!" exclaimed Thaddeus.

"I'll get her." Renee got up and headed to the door.

"You know what? I don't have to stand here and take this shit. I'm out of here!" Thaddeus exclaimed, as he walked toward the door.

"Go ahead and leave, you fuckin' liar!" Sheila yelled.

"You won't even let me get a word in, Sheila—to explain my side. You wanna believe everybody else."

"Who the fuck is everybody else? I'm getting this firsthand from my best friend, not everybody."

Thaddeus opened the door to leave.

"Yeah, but who is she getting it from?"

Renee walked back in the room with Trina and Kay Kay. They blocked Thaddeus from leaving the room.

Renee reintegrated what she said, "Like I said, Trina, we're not here to start no trouble. All we want is the truth and to clear shit up, okay?"

"Okay." Trina replied.

folding her arms with a smirk on her face.

"This is some kind of conspiracy type bullshit to break us up, Sheila. I've never touched that girl."

"Okay, Thaddeus. If you say so," said Trina.

"If he say so?" asked Sheila.

"Did he touch you or what, Trina?" Trina remained silent. Frustrated, Kay Kay blurted out.

"Yeah, he fucked her, touched her, whatever the fuck you want to call it! C'mon Trina...what you gonna sit here and lie for him for, after he denied you and your baby?"

"Oh, wow...a baby?" Sheila asked in disbelief.

"I'm sorry, Sheila. I didn't know you two were back together." Trina replied, as Thaddeus cut her off to intervene.

"She's a fuckin' liar, and I'm telling you right now in her face and yours, Sheila! She's just jealous of you and wants what you have."

"Oh, so you didn't fuck me in the shower about four or close to five months ago?"

Sheila started to tear up again and swung at Thaddeus. Trina, Kay Kay and Renee moved out of the way to keep from getting hit. Jim jumped and grabbed Sheila to try to bring some calm.

"Sheila, c'mon, sis. C'mon," Renee opened the door.

"Get the fuck out, Thaddeus! Thanks, Trina. Thanks, Kay Kay. Let us talk to Sheila, please."

Trina and Kay Kay leave out. Thaddeus, spoke out before leaving upset.

"Yeah, I guess y'all happy now, huh? Sheila, why you let them do this to us."

"Don't you dare say shit to her. Keep your ass movin' and get the fuck out!" exclaimed Renee.

Thaddeus left out slowly with a smirk on his face. Renee went over to hug her friend.

"I'm sorry it came out like this, Sheila."

Sheila cried.

"I couldn't let him keep playing you like that. I had to tell you."

"It's not your fault, Renee. You were only looking out for me. It was gonna hurt regardless how it came out. I'd rather it be from you, than to hear it from someone else."

Renee rolled off some toilet tissue and gave it to her.

"I can't believe I sucked his dick."

Jim cut in, "Well, that's my cue to go."

"Okay, Jim. I'll probably stay here tonight with Sheila and keep her company." Jim kissed Renee.

"That's only right, Babe. Call me later."

"Okay." Jim left out the door.

"You didn't tell me you went down on him! You must've really loved his ass."

"I did, and I was trying to prove to him how much I loved him."

"Did you even know how to do it?" Renee laughed, thinking devious thoughts. "You should've bit it off."

"After about the third time, I knew exactly what to do."

"Third time? Damn. You didn't even tell me? How did you know what to do?"

"Watching the porno Eric left here. Thaddeus taught me as well. Damn...Eric."

Sheila, looked down, sad.

"I bet this is my karma for what I did to him. I can't believe I hurt Eric like that. He was so good to me."

"Call him up. It's only been like three months."

"Naw. When we're in class, he acts like I don't even exist. I should've fixed it while I had the chance. I didn't have his back, so I know our relationship will never be the same."

"Well, you never know what can happen."

"Don't say anything to him, Renee."

"Who said I was going to say something?"

Renee looked away from Sheila.

"Nobody. I just know you. Don't say anything."

"Alright, alright. I won't. Let's put a movie or something on to take your mind off things."

"I don't care. Do whatever."

"What you wanna watch?"

"Eric's movie."

"I should've known, you little freak." Renee laughed.

"Whew! Let me lay down. All this excitement got my damn back hurting."

"Renee. I have a question?"

"What's up?"

"You've been getting sick a lot lately. When was the last time you had a period?"

Renee started to think with a puzzled look.

Renee, Jim, and Sheila walk into the clinic to the Reception Desk. The receptionist greets them.

"Hello. How may I help you?"

"Hi." Renee replied.

"My girlfriend is here to see the doctor," Sheila said. Jim cut in,

"No, we are here to see the doctor."

"All of you?" asked the receptionist.

"No, Miss. These two are here to see the doctor, and I'm just here for support," Sheila clarified.

"Okay, thanks for clearing that up for me. Have you ever been here before?"

"No," Renee replied.

"Do you have insurance?"

"Yes. It's right here."

Renee handed over the insurance card to the receptionist.

"And what are you here for?"

Renee whispered, "Pregnancy test."

"Excuse me, I didn't hear you?"

"We need a pregnancy test." Jim said clearly.

"I can't believe Ms. Big Mouth can't speak the hell up for some reason," said Sheila.

"I'm sorry. I'm just scared, y'all. I never had to go to the clinic for something like this before."

The receptionist handed her back her card.

"Okay, here's your card back. I need you to fill out these forms. When you are done, bring them back up to me."

Renee, Jim, and Sheila took a seat and started looking around the clinic to see who else was in there.

"Why do they ask so many questions to get a pregnancy test? I don't know anything about my mom or dad's health?"

"Just answer the best way you know how, Babe," Jim replied.

"I'm just gonna write that they are healthy, point blank. Oh my God, are they gonna tell my parents?"

"I don't know." Sheila replied.

"You want me to ask?" asked Jim.

"Yes, please, Babe."

Jim went back up to the receptionist.

"Sheila, I don't know if this is a good idea…"

"Just wait, Renee, before you start to panic. See what she says."

Jim walked back.

"She said they don't tell them because you are of age, but then she did say there's a possibility the insurance company could send them an invoice."

"Oh, shit. I change my mind."

Jim grabbed her and pulled her back to her seat.

"Renee, c'mon. Let's get this over with. If you are, either way, they are going to find out."

"No, they won't."

"Yes, they will. What? Are you gonna stay away from them until the baby is born?"

"No. You're gonna give me some money for an abortion."

"No, the fuck I ain't!"

Everyone in the clinic got quiet and all eyes were on them. Sheila put her index finger to her lips and got in between them.

"Shhhh…," she whispered. "Y'all don't even know if she is pregnant or not, and already you are arguing."

Jim started arguing in a whisper tone.

"She's talkin' about killing my fuckin' baby."

Renee argued back in the same whisper tone.

"It's not a baby yet, Jim."

"It's life!" Jim got up and walked out.

"You done with those papers, Renee?" Sheila asked.

"Yeah."

"Give them here, so I can take them up."

Before Sheila could sit back down, they called Renee.

"Go ahead, Renee. I'll go out and get Jim."

Sheila went out and got Jim. They both went back in and headed toward the back, when the nurse stopped them.

"I'm sorry, but only one can go in the back at this time." Sheila stopped.

"You go, Jim, and please try to refrain from arguing back there."

Jim looked angry, as he followed the nurse into the room. Renee was in the bathroom.

"She's in the bathroom. She should be right out."

"Okay, thank you." Renee came out of the bathroom holding a cup of urine and stood at the door with it. The nurse walked up to Renee and retrieved the cup.

"Jim, I'm sorry. I didn't mean to upset you like that." Jim was quiet.

"You ain't saying anything I want to hear right now, Renee."

"What do you want to hear, Jim?"

"That you are keeping my baby."

"Jim, my parents will kill me if I'm pregnant!"

"No, they won't."

"Yes, they will."

"They will have to go through me first."

"Jim, what are you going to do? Beat my parents up?"

"When you're talking about mine, yeah…if I have to."

"Jim, you are talking about my parents."

"And you are talking about my child."

The nurse entered the room.

"Okay, I need to draw some blood from you."

"Draw some blood?"

"Yes, ma'am."

The nurse prepped everything she needed, tied Renee's arm with a big rubber band, cleaned it with alcohol, and proceeded to draw blood.

"Okay, you're going to feel a little pinch."

"Oh God, hurry, I already feel faint." Renee said.

"Okay, all done."

"Whew, thank you! I need to take a nap after that."

"Well, you don't have that long to sleep because the doctor will be in shortly," the nurse replied.

"Okay."

The doctor walked in shortly after the nurse left.

"Hello, Ms. Williams. I am Doctor Kline. How are you today?"

"Good, but I can be great if I'm not pregnant."

"Well, what kind of precautions did you take to avoid getting pregnant?"

"None," replied Renee.

"Well, I guess we are just going to have to settle with being "good" because your pregnancy test is positive."

"What?"

Renee started crying, and Jim moved closer to hug her.

"Do you know when your last menstrual cycle was? You said on your history form, you weren't sure, and to get an idea of how far along you are, I need that to help."

"I think it was during break…" Renee answered

"I think you are right, Renee," Jim intervened.

"You were mad your mom didn't have any pads at the house; there were only tampons."

"So, would you say that was roughly about five, six months ago?" asked Dr. Kline.

"Yeah, about six months," Jim replied.

"Shit! That bitch been missing that long?!" Renee exclaimed surprisingly.

"Do you feel any kind of movement, Renee?"

"Gas."

"Any changes with your breasts?"

"Ummm…I haven't noticed."

"Yes, she was complaining about them hurting and her nipples are appearing to get darker," Jim replied.

"They are?" Renee asked Jim.

"Yes, Renee," replied Jim.

"Okay, so what we are going to do is set you up with an ultrasound to

114

get measurements of the baby and an accurate due date for you. For now, I'll do an internal exam to get somewhat of an idea."

He reached for his gloves.

"Okay," Renee replied.

"Now, just lie back, place your feet in the stirrups, slide all the way down, and open your legs. You will feel a lubricant on my fingers, as I start to insert them."

Renee talked to Jim as she held his hand through the exam.

"I can't believe this shit, Jim. This is a damn nightmare."

She started to cry.

"I'm not hurting you, am I?" asked Dr. Kline.

"No. I'm just a little upset."

"Okay, all done. You can slide back up on the bed now. By the feel of things, I would say you are around five months."

"What?!" Jim and Renee replied in unison.

"Five months?" Jim repeated again.

"Yes. The nurse will come in with your scheduled ultrasound, and please give the office a call in about two days to follow up on your test results."

"Okay," Renee said, still in disbelief.

"I hope everything works out for the both of you. Nice meeting you two. Enjoy your day."

"Thank you, Dr. Kline," they both replied.

Renee, Sheila, and Jim are waiting patiently for the ultrasound technician to come in for the ultrasound.

"Hello! I see we have a full house! My name is Sarah."

"Hi, Sarah," everyone spoke.

"I'll be doing your ultrasound today. Have you ever had one?"

"No," Renee replied.

"Okay, just lay back. I am gonna put a warm gel on your abdominal area and roll this thing called a Transducer Probe on top of it, so we can peep into the baby's home. Are you ready?"

"Yes, we're ready."

As the technician began, everyone looked at the screen. They saw black and white but were not clear what they were actually seeing, yet. As they focused, a clearer image started to come through. Jim jumped up.

"Oh my God!"

"That's a whole baby in there!" Renee said excitingly. Look at it, Jim. It's playing and everything."

Jim started biting his bottom lip, trying to not tear up.

"Renee, you can't feel that?" Sheila asked.

"Yes, I can feel it. I thought it was gas all this time. I blamed it on Hardee's and the cafeteria food."

"Well, as you see, it's not gas." Renee looked at Jim and started tearing up with him.

"See, Renee, it's a baby—our baby."

"Yes, it is. I didn't know that babies actually did all this while inside the belly."

"Do you want to know what it is?" asked the technician

"Oh my God, yes! You can actually tell us that?"

"I hope it's a girl." Renee said a prayer.

"I don't care what it is. I just hope it's healthy and she has it," said Jim.

"I'm not gonna get rid of our baby, Jim. I love my baby already."

Jim, overwhelmed with happiness, hugged and kissed her, as the technician interrupted.

"Okay, we have to hurry with the sex and measurements, you guys. Can you lay back, all the way, again for me, Renee?"

The technician rolled, clicked, and began to type a few times.

"Okay, you're 26 weeks, and it's a girl."

Everyone cheered as Renee and Jim teared up with joy.

"Jasmine," Renee said excitedly.

"Jasmine?" Sheila asked.

"Yup, that's what I'm gonna name her."

Jim started talkin' to her stomach.

"Hey, Jasmine, baby. Daddy loves you."

They all giggled.

"Okay, get dressed, and I'll have some pictures of Jasmine for you to take home before you leave," the technician said happily.

"Awww, thank you so much!"

Renee and Jim were full of gratitude, as they received their pictures.

"Girl, I can't believe how much Jasmine moved around in your stomach," Sheila said.

"I know! Me either. Looking from the outside, it doesn't even look like anything is in my stomach, but then when you look inside, she's at her own playground."

They all laughed.

"I can't believe I'm gonna be a father. I definitely gotta bust my ass to get in the NFL," Jim said.

"You already got that, Baby. The teams are pretty much fighting over you now."

Renee cheering him on.

"And you best believe, I'm gonna take good care of my two little women." He kissed Renee.

Renee and Sheila are chilling in the room. There's a hard, panicked knock at the door. Renee and Sheila jump up as Sheila opens the door.

"Who the fuck is it?"

Mr. and Mrs. Williams stormed in their room. Mrs. Williams grabbed Renee by her hair and pulled her down. Sheila stood there in shock.

"We're not paying for you to be up here fuckin'. We're paying for you to go to college to get a damn education!"

Sheila jumped up and yelled.

"Mrs. Williams, stop it! She's pregnant!"

"Don't you think I know that, Sheila?!" Mrs. Williams still held Renee down by her hair while yelling.

"Your grown ass is up here making babies?!"

"I'm sorry, Mom. I didn't know!' Renee cried. "What the hell didn't you know—that you were pregnant or that you could get pregnant? What the hell you didn't know?"

Mr. Williams tried to get his wife off Renee.

"Come on, Honey. Let her up."

"Pack your shit! You're leaving!"

"I'm gonna need a couple of days to pack, Mom."

"No, you don't. Here are some bags. Put your shit in, and let's go!"

"Where's Jim?" asked Mr. Williams.

"He's at practice," Renee replied.

"I'm going to head on over to the field and have a little talk with Mr. Jim. I'll be right back, Honey."

"Why, Dad?" asked Renee, as Mrs. Williams cut her off.

"None of your damn business! Now pack!"

Mr. Williams leaves out and gets in the car to drive over to the football field. Mr. Williams proceeds to walk onto the field, toward the team's practice. Jim tries to make out if he is seeing clearly that Mr. Williams is coming across the field. Once the visual is confirmed, and Jim realizes it's him, Jim immediately stops practice and runs over.

"I would shake your hand, but I'm a bit dirty from practicing. Are you here to give me your blessing?"

"No. You're lucky I don't punch you in your damn mouth, but there are too many witnesses out here. I'm here to take my daughter back home," Mr. Williams replied.

All of a sudden, Jim took off running to Renee's dorm. Mr. Williams jumped back into his car to follow him. Jim took a shortcut through the school and ran by Mr. Williams, as he pulled up and parked his car. Jim ran non-stop to beat him to Renee's dorm. Jim knocked in a panic.

"Renee!" Sheila got up and opened the door.

"Renee stop packing. You ain't going nowhere!"

Mrs. Williams gets in his face.

"This is my daughter, and I said she's coming home."

Jim replied to Mrs. Williams, as Mr. Williams walks in, "She is carrying my daughter, and I said she's not!"

"Man, have you lost your mind? That's my wife you're talking to, and this here is my family" Mr. Williams said, pointing at Mrs. Williams and Renee.

"You're out of line and being disrespectful."

"I'm not trying to be disrespectful, Mr. and Mrs. Williams. I'm trying to save my family just like you."

"As I told you on the phone, you're not ready for a family. You two are kids, and you're too young to be getting married and thinking about kids," Mr. Williams replied in Jim's face.

Renee is surprised at what she just heard.

"On the phone?"

They ignore Renee and keep talking.

"Next year, I will be playing for the NFL."

"Man, that's not a guarantee. What if, tomorrow you break a knee, your back, shoulder, or whatever? You are done!" exclaimed Mr. Williams.

"That's not going to happen..."

"You can't guarantee that. Football is football, and it's a competitive, contact sport. Anything can happen! And once that happens, then what?"

"I have contracts and endorsements knocking on my door now. We'll be okay," replied Jim.

"That's your money. We need our daughter to be an independent, strong woman. I don't want her to depend on no one for nothing, waiting around for you to get a check."

"It wouldn't be like that, and you know it," Jim replied.

"That's the problem. I don't know. Anything can change, especially after you receive that contract. You'll be in the limelight, with money, women, and flashy cars—you name it. You're not going to be thinking about my daughter. Marrying her because she's pregnant," Renee intervened.

"Marrying me?"

Jim turned around to Renee and held her hand.

"Yes, Baby. That's why your parents are here. I told them you were pregnant, and that I wanted to do the right thing by asking for your hand in marriage."

"Let's do it, Jim," Renee said.

"You ain't doing shit!" Mrs. Williams jumped in.

"Please, don't talk to her like that," Jim replied as Mr. Williams intervened.

"Jim, this is between my wife and my daughter. I suggest you stay out of it."

"And my soon-to-be wife. I love her, and I wanted to marry her long before finding out she was carrying my daughter."

Mrs. Williams looked surprised.

"How do you know it's a girl?"

"We had an ultrasound done. Here, look at her pictures."

Mr. and Mrs. Williams looked at the pictures of their granddaughter. Mrs. Williams turned to Renee.

"Oh, you're that far along, Renee?"

"Yes," Renee replied.

"So, it may be too late for a damn abortion?"

"Abortion?! Over my dead body! That's my child, and I wish you would try to abort my baby," Jim said angrily.

Renee and Mr. Williams jumped between Jim and Mrs. Williams. Mr. Williams pushed Jim back out of his wife's face, as their argument turned into a tussle, pushing Renee out of the way. Renee yelled and let out a horrible cry.

"Stop! Just stop it! Please!" Jim stopped immediately and ran over to help Renee.

"I'm sorry. You okay, Baby?"

Renee cried as Jim held her. Mrs. Williams was breathing hard and held her husband, who was also breathing hard from the scuffle.

"Come on, Renee. Get the rest of your shit, and let's go!" exclaimed Mrs. Williams.

"No!" Renee replied.

"What the fuck did you just say to me?"

"I said no, Mom!" Renee mustered through her tears.

"My life may not be going in the direction you want it to go, but it's still my life. I'm going to have my baby and marry Jim. I'm old enough and don't need your consent to do so," cried Renee.

"You want to be grown? Okay, be grown—your money stops here. Your tuition stops here. Your home—you are no longer welcome, and don't you dare even think about lifting a finger to call me to ask for shit!" Mr. Williams screams in anger.

He and Mrs. Williams grabbed their things and left out the door. Renee started crying.

"I can't believe I disrespected my parents like that."

"You didn't disrespect them. You stood up to them," Jim replied, holding her.

"What am I going to do now? They've cut me off of everything."

"Don't worry about it, Baby. I'm gonna take care of you. Let me call my parents. I'll get us an apartment close by to the school, and we'll commute back and forth until we finish out the school year."

As Jim continued to talk, Renee screamed.

"What the fuck is this?!"

She looked down at her sweats. They were saturated with a liquid substance between her legs.

"Did I just pee myself?" asked Renee.

"Eww, yuck! What is that?" asked Sheila.

"Ouch!" cried Renee.

"What? Are you feeling pain? Sit down."

Sheila and Jim catered to her needs.

"Yes, it's starting to feel like I'm cramping. Ouch! Omg! It's starting to hurt really bad."

Renee started crying.

"That doesn't sound right, Renee."

Sheila yelled, "Call 9-1-1, Jim!"

Jim jumped up to grab the phone to call 9-1-1. Sheila noticed a faint showing of blood starting to mix with the liquid substance between her legs.

"Tell them to hurry, Jim!" Sheila yelled.

"Oh my God! It's really starting to hurt now!"

Jim ran back over to help lay her down. He repeated what the emergency responder said to him over the phone.

"They told me to make sure you are off your feet, to lay you back in an upright position, and to elevate your feet until they arrive."

"Ouch!" Renee continued to feel the pain.

"Baby, please try to relax."

"I can't. It hurts so bad. Take me to the bathroom. I gotta poop."

"I don't think that's a good idea. They told me to make sure you stay put and to lay you down."

"Give me something to poop in.

Sheila and Jim started looking around for something.

"Sheila take my pants off, please."

Sheila helped take her pants off, as the EMTs arrived with a knock at the door, asking to come inside. Jim opened the door.

"She said she's having a real bad cramping pain, and she's gotta poop!" exclaimed Sheila to the EMTs.

"How many weeks is she?" the EMTs asked, putting on gloves to assess her and to take her vitals.

"Twenty-six," Jim replied.

"Oh, shit! It really, really hurts. I gotta go to the bathroom, now!" Renee yelled crying and in pain.

"Renee, it appears that your water broke. Open wide, so I can see if you're dilated."

Renee opened her legs wide for the EMTs.

"She is in active labor. Renee, please do not push. We have to get you to the hospital," said the EMT assessing her.

"But I've got to poop!" Renee exclaimed.

"It's not poop you're feeling, Renee. You're feeling pressure from the baby. It's too soon to push right now, so please, whatever you do, try not to push. We are going to get you to the hospital as soon as possible."

"Wait, what?! It's too soon, right?" cried Renee.

Jim and Sheila were in a panic, holding Renee's hands as she continued to cry.

"I'll hold her. I'll hold her, Jim! I don't want to lose my Jasmine!"

The other EMT brought up the bed.

"Okay, Renee. I am going to transfer you over to the other bed and get you to the hospital."

They count: "One…two…three."

They lifted her to transfer her over to the other bed and strapped Renee down. Then, they proceeded to take her straight to the hospital.

"Will one of you be riding?" asked the EMT.

"Jim, you go. I'll see if I can get someone to bring me and meet you there," Sheila replied.

Shelia arrives at the hospital with Kelly about forty-five minutes to an hour later. The nurse shows her to Renee's room, where Jim's head is down on the pure white sheets, holding Renee's hand. Renee is lying back, her eyes filled with water and the bed half-raised. Sheila tiptoes in and quietly enters the dim room.

"Hey...how's everything, Renee? Is everything okay?"

As she opened her eyes, a big tear rolled down her face. Jim lifted his head with a red face, as tears flowed down his face.

"She's gone, Sheila."

Renee cried uncontrollably.

"What do you mean, she's gone, Renee? We just met her." Sheila started to cry.

"My Jasmine is gone," cried out Renee.

They both hugged each other and let out a big cry. Jim joined in and hugged them both.

"I can't believe she's gone, Renee. Jasmine. Jasmine..."

Jim got up and walked out, as they continued to cry. Renee was worried about Jim's well-being.

"Sheila, check on Jim for me. Make sure he doesn't snap, please."

"Okay, Renee."

Renee continued to cry but called Sheila back.

"Sheila, will you call Matt, please?

"Matt?" Sheila asked confused.

"Yes...can you tell him I'm sorry, and let him know I know what it's like now."

Renee rolled over, pulled the covers over her head, and continued to cry.

To Be Continued...
Vol 2: The Lifestyle Series - The Secret Sexual Society

THE LIFESTYLE

VOLUME 3

What's your SeXual Desire?

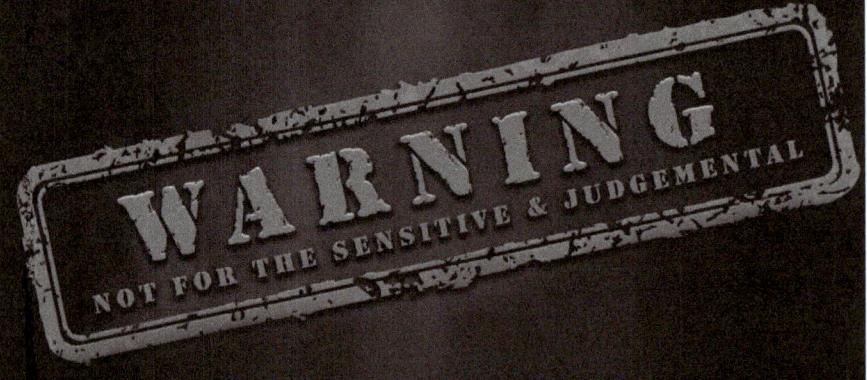

WARNING

NOT FOR THE SENSITIVE & JUDGEMENTAL

Y. MONEY